BARLEY BREAD AND CHEESE

A collection of short stories
inspired by
Rochester Cathedral and its treasures

By

T. Thurai

First edition published 2013
Published by: Hot Monkey Publishing
Email address: contact@hotmonkeypublishing.com
Copyright © T. Thurai 2013

DISCLAIMER
All characters in this book are entirely fictional and any similarity between any of them and real individuals is entirely coincidental and unintentional.

THE AUTHOR'S WEBSITE:
Additional information about the author and her work can be found at: www.thedevildancers.com

THE AUTHOR'S BLOG
The author's blog can be found at:
                    http://tthurai.wordpress.com/

For Joan, Indra and Rohan

Index

Introduction

There is a piece of advice that is common currency among all writers: as soon as you have finished your first book, you must begin your second.

I had finished writing my first novel *The Devil Dancers*. A modern historical novel set in 1950s Ceylon, it had set me an extraordinary challenge. I not only had to write about the past but also another country. The result was nine years' gruelling research and writing.

Having finished *The Devil Dancers* – and following the popular dictum – I immediately embarked on another historical novel: this time set in World War II. This was intended to be my second book. However, I was led astray. And Mr Dickens was to blame!

Intrigued by references to Ceylon in *The Mystery of Edwin Drood*, I visited Rochester Cathedral – the main setting for Dickens's fictitious town of Cloisterham. What I discovered inspired me to write *The Cinnamon Peeler's Daughter*: a story that became the keystone for this collection.

Such is the power of literature! Exactly 150 years after his death, Dickens had introduced me to the inspiration for this book: Rochester Cathedral. The more I visited it, the more I wanted to know. The more I read, the more intrigued I became.

Of course, it is principally a place of worship. But Rochester Cathedral is also a repository for historical and artistic treasures of national importance; some well-known, others less so.

Using some of these treasures as my starting point, I began to sketch out a number of short stories. The result was *Barley Bread and Cheese*: a book that combines fiction with brief historical insights. Each story is accompanied by a short description of the treasure that inspired it. By including some factual information, I hope to inspire readers to discover more about Rochester Cathedral and its extraordinary history.

The journey has been a fascinating one. I have learned much and met some wonderful people, especially the staff and volunteers of Rochester Cathedral. I would like to thank them all for their warm welcome, support and generosity. My thanks also to Mr Dickens.

Now, I really must return to that other novel!

T. Thurai
30th June 2013

The Broken Wing

The Treasure: Bishop Hamo's Archway

Stories are all around us, waiting to be told. But sometimes we need a helping hand.

For several months, elements of this story had been swirling about in my mind. It had been sparked off by an incident with a bird's wing at my mother's house, similar to that experienced by the narrator at the beginning of the story. However, it was only after a visit to Rochester Cathedral that the story took shape.

During that visit, I was approached by one of the Cathedral's volunteers, a former guide, who kindly introduced me to some of the less well-known features of this beautiful building.

Among these was a detail on the elaborate archway constructed in 1343 at the behest of Bishop Hamo de Hythe. Located in the South Quire Transept, this elaborately carved doorway provided access to the Cathedral for monks from the Benedictine priory.

My guide told me to look closely at the inner register of the archway. Here you will find a row of cherubs' faces, becoming increasingly cheerful as they ascend. At the apex of this inner band of decoration is what appears to be the sculpture of a naked child which represents Bishop Hamo's soul rising to heaven.

Soon afterwards, I awoke one morning with the plot of my story complete and the voice of its narrator ringing in my ears. Strangely, it was not a Kentish voice, but one from the north of England. Ultimately it was to lead me to another angelic figure: the Angel of the North.

The Broken Wing

The house was as still as a tomb. Lying awake in the half-light, I listened for the first sounds of morning. The high-pitched whine of the milk-float, the clang of my gate as it hit the wall, the clink of bottles being placed, none too carefully, on my step. Then, an hour or two later, the faint twitter of birds followed by the rumble of traffic.

Every morning, I listened, hoping for a sign, a token of change. But it never came. Each day was like the last. I would reach my hand across the bed and feel only the cold silence of the sheets. The space, that had once shaped itself around the contours of a body, had collapsed: flat, cold, empty.

No, this day would be like all the rest.

I lay there thinking. Of nothing.

I reached for the button on the radio. More death and disaster. I switched it off again. There are worse things than silence.

I grappled with the sheets and blankets that ensnared me; grumbling as I struggled with their warm coils. Then, breathless, I sat on the edge of the bed, my toes playing hide-and-seek with my slippers.

No.

I closed my eyes, bracing myself for the day ahead: a day that held no hope, no expectation. I would have welcomed a challenge. Even an argument with a tax official or a council clerk would have relieved the tedium. But, since Aggie's death, every day had been a flatline.

A dove began to coo. It must have settled on the chimney because the whole house began to reverberate with its noise; a soft, insistent lullaby. I felt a quickening of my heart. Nothing to do with angina; but something more pleasant. The sort of feeling you get on a May morning. When, just as you are waking, cool air from the garden breathes on your face.

I shuffled downstairs, hanging onto the banisters, noticing how big the knuckles on my fingers were getting, how white and cold the skin looked. Despite the central heating, I always felt cold in the mornings; never warming up until my first cup of tea.

I went straight to the kitchen with its bleak expanse of grey linoleum. A bad choice. Mine. Aggie had wanted cream, but I had objected arguing that it was impractical. As usual, she had deferred.

"Oh well, Fred. You know best."

I didn't. But I only realised after she had gone.

12

Aggie had been the one with all the answers. I should have listened.

I filled the kettle and flicked the switch. It activated a bright light like a gas flame: ~~old gas, the sort that used to kill you~~. But not even suicide was easy any longer. After Aggie's death, I had calculated how many shops I would have to visit to buy enough aspirin to do the job properly. Too many.

I hadn't the energy. Dying was too much trouble. So I'd hung on here, alone: dreading the dawn and the continuation of life that was no longer mine to enjoy. The worst thing about loss is not grief: it's the lack of joy; the endless numbness.

Loading my cereal and tea onto the trolley, I pushed it into the lounge. The curtains were drawn and the room was still dark. Sometimes, I left it like that. It felt safe. Like being in a burrow, disconnected from the world outside.

Wallowing in artificial night, I sat down to drink my tea. But I could not find the deathly peace that I craved. Amplified by the fire-place, the dove's persistent cooing had become even louder.

"Coo-cooooo. Coo-cooooo."

This was followed by some scratching and rustling, then another sound; a passionate throaty gurgling. The dove had found a mate.

Not sure the story needs this bit about the doves.

13

"Shut up!" I shouted to the fire-place. "Shut up!"

But after a moment's silence, they were at it again, louder than ever.

"I'll put a stop to that," I yelled. "Just you wait."

My plan was to go into the garden through the French doors and hurl some clods of earth and stones up at the chimney. Rummaging through a drawer stuffed with old cheque books and gas bills, I found the key. I hadn't opened those doors for ages. Not since Aggie died.

Flinging back the curtains, I was about to insert the key into the lock when something caught my eye. Close up, it looked like two huge puffs of dust, covering the French windows. I took a step back, then another. From a few feet away, it looked like the imprint of two gigantic wings.

I'd seen something like it before when a pigeon or some smaller bird had flown into the window. They usually died instantly from a broken neck or from shock a day or two later. I'd tried to revive a blackbird once, keeping it warm in a box of hay. After scrabbling about feebly, it had watched me quietly and I had seen its eye dim as the spirit departed. Just as I had done with Aggie.

I opened the doors and inspected the window

from outside. I dabbed at the imprint and inspected the dust sparkling on the tip of my finger. Powder down: the stuff that coats birds' feathers. They were definitely wings. But huge.

I was wondering what kind of bird could have left this impression, when I heard a noise behind me. Turning, I peered down the garden and saw a huddle of white feathers lying on the lawn.

"Oh my god," I muttered. "It must be a swan."

I found a small rake propped up by the door and using it for support I walked slowly down the garden to where the bird lay.

As I got closer, I could see one great wing at full stretch. The bird seemed to have curled up inside it. I could not see a beak, or a neck or even a webbed foot. It must have been very badly injured. Or perhaps, the fox had got at it in the night. Only I couldn't see the usual trail of feathers left by scavengers.

As I got closer, the wing trembled.

"Oh no, it's still alive," I murmured.

I'd have to call the Council. Or the RSPCA. Swans were protected birds, belonging to the Crown. I certainly wasn't going to finish it off. I might end up in jail.

There was a low moan. Almost human. I took a step closer. The wing trembled again and then a boy's head appeared from one end and a foot from the other.

"Oh, me 'ead," he moaned.

"What are you doing out here under that swan's wing?" I demanded.

The boy moaned again. A hand appeared from under the wing and started rubbing his scalp. I stepped closer. He looked familiar. I fumbled about in my pockets, looking for my specs. When I pushed them on my nose, my hand was trembling. I edged closer. Took another look. There was no mistake.

"Joey?" I gasped. "Joey Williams. It can't be."

"It is", he said, looking up at me with bloodshot eyes.

"But ... but you're dead!"

"Tell me about it," he groaned. "First that motorbike and now this. Seems I can't stop crashing into things."

Clutching his head with both hands, Joey rolled onto his back. He was naked, except for a pair of feathery drawers, his skin covered in a strange, glistening down. A boy with enormous wings.

My legs turned to jelly and I had to cling onto the rake for support. I was seeing things. No doubt about it. I must have accidentally taken too many pills. Or perhaps I was having a turn.

It couldn't be Joey. He'd died a couple of days ago. Road accident. He had lived in the next street. Aggie and I had known him since he was a baby. She'd had a real soft spot for him; would have been distraught if she'd still been around. But she wasn't. She'd been gone five years. *— too long — a year?*

The boy moaned.

A hallucination. I'd prove it. I prodded him with my foot.

"Ow! What are you kicking me for?"

He rolled back onto his side, groaning. He looked just like Joey.

"I've hurt me wing."

He spoke like Joey, too. *what do you mean you're — who are you — what are you eh?*

"Let me take a look."

I knew a bit about wings having kept pigeons as a boy. I lowered myself slowly, first one knee, then the other, felt the joints crack and wondered how I'd get up again.

Placing my hands under the wing, I extended it gently, feeling for breaks.

"Ow! Ooh-hoo-hoo!" yelled Joey.

"Quiet," I hissed. "You'll wake the neighbours."

"Who cares? They never liked me anyway."

"They never liked your bike," I corrected. "What do you expect? Revving it up under their window at all hours. Since they got the news of your accident, she hasn't stopped crying."

"Really?"

His face brightened. He looked pleased. Selfish little sod.

"Yes, really."

I tweaked his wing and he winced.

"It's not too bad. It'll soon mend. Just needs a few days' rest."

"A few days! But where will I go?"

"Back to your parents."

"I can't do that."

"Why not?"

"It's not allowed."

"Not allowed? By whom?"

"It's one of the rules. If I want to keep me wings, I can't go back. Not now."

"Well ... I don't know what to suggest."

"Can I stay here?"

"With me?"

"Yeah. Just until I can fly again. They wouldn't mind that."

"They? Who's they? And why wouldn't they mind?"

"Because ...," he stammered and blushed. "Because ..."

"Go on, lad. Spit it out."

"Because everyone thinks you're a daft old man. No-one will believe what you say."

"Oh, like that is it?"

Pulling myself up with the rake, I stumped off up the path. There was a frantic fluttering: a commotion of feathers. The boy had got to his feet and was running after me.

"Please. I didn't mean to offend you. It's not what *I* think. It's just what *they* said. *"If you have an accident, ask someone to take you in. An old person, living on their own. They're the best."* And, it was in your garden it happened."

"You flew into my windows. You young vandal."

"No. It wasn't like that. I was with the Flight. On practice. I'm still not used to it yet. I was falling behind, couldn't keep up. They're that fast you see. But they said if ever I got lost to fly towards the sun. So I did. But I didn't realise, it was the sun's reflection. In your windows. I hit 'em with a right wallop."

"I should say. Cracked one of them right across. It'll cost me a fortune to replace."

"I'm sorry. Really."

A dog growled menacingly. Next door's Staffordshire. I could hear it snuffling under the fence. Then I heard voices.

"What's up, Tobin? Can you smell a rabbit?"

The dog began to bay, scratching frantically at the fence.

"Please," begged Joey. "Hide me. Just for a while."

I sighed. But I knew what Aggie would have done.

"All right. In you come."

Even with both French windows open, Joey had to squeeze himself into the small front room. When I offered him an armchair he refused.

"I can't. It's me wings. They won't fit. I'll just perch here if you don't mind."

And he sat on the table. The down on his skin glistened in the sunlight, glowing like a halo.

I could see that his teeth were chattering. I felt sorry for him. He was only a kid. And he looked lost.

"Tell you what. I'll make us both a cup of tea and you can tell me what happened."

"Thanks."

"Fancy a piece of toast?"

"No, I can't."

"Can't?"

"Not able to eat any more. Just water. But tea would be OK. I'd like that."

Shaking my head, I shuffled into the kitchen. Nothing surprised me any more. I'd lived through the war and all the bombing. Some strange things happened then. And Aggie. Sitting with her, day after day, holding her hand, praying for a miracle which never came.

Strange how the miracles that do come are never the ones you want. And they're inconvenient. Like this lad. How was I going to keep it quiet? What did I tell his parents? They'd have to be told, of course.

I foraged in the china-cupboard for the best mugs, the flowery ones that Aggie and I had always used. They were a bit dusty, but responded well to a bit of soap and water. It felt good making tea again in those mugs. Like old times. I set everything out on the trolley: doilies, tea-plates, mugs of tea, sugar, the Apostle spoons. Just like Aggie did.

"Sure you won't have a biscuit?"

I offered him a digestive, but it turned him green.

"No thanks."

"Let's take a look at that wing."

He drew away, a little scared.

"Don't worry. I grew up mending birds' wings. There aren't many I've not fixed; peregrine falcon, pigeon, blackbird."

"But not an angel's?"

He smirked.

"Is that what you are? It's not what I heard your dad call you when you first came off that bike. Silly young sod, that's what he called you."

"I know."

He giggled. Still a kid, awkward and a bit embarrassed.

"He never wanted me to have that bike."

"With good reason as it turns out."

"I know. I'm sorry. It was all my fault. Going too fast."

"Yes, well ... at least no-one else was hurt."

"No. I wouldn't have had these if they had been. Not straight off. I'd had to have worked a lot harder."

"Yes, I'll say that for you. You were always a hard worker. Builder weren't you?"

"Plasterer's mate."

He fell silent, reflecting on his old life. As he sat quietly, I took the opportunity to inspect his wings. There wasn't much damage – a few flight feathers snapped and bent that would soon re-grow. It was shock more than anything else.

I tried to straighten the feathers out. They felt soft, silky; different from bird's feathers. Even lighter, if that were possible. And they had a kind of translucent glow.

I had nearly finished working on his wing, when there was a knock at the door.

"You wait here," I warned him. "And don't make a sound."

I tried to shut the living-room door behind me but, as usual, it stuck leaving a narrow opening. Muttering, I began the ritual of opening the front door, sliding back the bolt, taking the chain off the hook, unlocking it. I usually did this first thing after getting up; but nothing today had followed the usual pattern.

"Like Fort Knox," said a cheery voice as I opened the door.

It was Dave the postman, a nice enough fellow but a bit nosey.

I took a parcel from him – a pair of slippers I'd ordered over the internet. As I did so, there was a crash from the room behind me.

"What's going on in there?" said Dave, peering over my shoulder.

"Ferret," I said.

"Ferret? But I thought I heard something flapping. Like wings."

"Pigeon," I said.

"A ferret and a pigeon! Out together! You'd better watch it, Fred. Leave 'em alone any longer and you won't have a pigeon. Just a fat ferret."

He laughed at his own joke. I smiled sourly and shut the door quicker than was polite.

Back in the front room, I found the boy standing in front of the fire-place, apologetic.

"Sorry. I got cramp. I don't know how to control these things yet. I knocked over one of your ornaments."

It was a vase, cheap and ugly, but one which I had won with Aggie when we had visited a fair in our courting days.

"Silly idiot," I thought.

He bent over to pick up the pieces and swept something else off the mantelpiece.

"Stop, stop. You're wrecking my house. I'll do it. You just sit still."

I picked up the pieces and put them on the table in a pile. I'm not usually sentimental but I couldn't bring myself to throw them away.

***

There were a lot of breakages that week: vases, dinner-plates, a tea-pot, even one of Aggie's flowery mugs. That upset me. But he couldn't help it. His wings kept knocking things over. Even folded, they reached to the ceiling and when he yawned, or coughed, or got cramp they would stretch out of their own accord, filling the whole room.

The only time he was really safe was when he was asleep, curled up inside the great white wings like a small child, a gentle smile on his face. Then, I'd just sit, watching him for hours. Like he was my own. We'd never had a child and having him here seemed to fill an ache that I never realised I'd had.

Not until now.

Having him around the house seemed quite natural. But there was one thing that bothered me.

"Why're you wearing kecks, Joey. It doesn't quite fit with my idea of an angel."

He blushed.

"Well, most of them go commando. You know. No pants at all. I mean, you don't have 'parts' up there. There's no gender, no men and women, so it doesn't matter. But I couldn't get used to the idea. So they let me hang on to me Y-fronts for a while. Just until I got used to it."

"Oh right."

I began to ?? time with Aggie.

I remembered a time with Aggie when alone in the sand-dunes at Amble Links we had stripped off all our clothes and laid in the sun. Then, in a secluded hollow screened by sea-grass, we had made love, to the sound of the sea. It was the closest I had ever been to heaven.

"You'll see her again, you know."

The boy patted my hand.

"How did you know ...?"

27

"I can read your thoughts."

He giggled.

"Who'd 'a thought it of you, Fred Turner. Never thought of you and Aggie doing things like that."

"That's enough," I shouted. "Me thoughts are me own. You stay out of 'em."

"Sorry."

He blushed again and hung his head.

"It's all right," I relented. "I wouldn't have had that memory if it hadn't 'a been for you."

He hugged himself, grinning.

"Great. All I want to do is help. That's what it's like now. Just thinking of others. Not yourself. It's nice. Makes you feel lighter somehow."

I understood. Because I had begun to feel lighter too. The heaviness of grief had begun to lift. Colours seemed brighter and small things that I had overlooked now had the power to make me gasp in amazement.

Flowers, feathers, birds' eggs – all appeared miraculous. Simple things became objects of wonder. The mundane became extraordinary.

Strangely, I no longer needed my glasses. It was as if I had a new set of eyes – a child's eyes – and I was seeing everything for the first time.

***

But then I had to let him go. His wing had healed and he was getting anxious.

"Do you think I'll be able to fly again?"

"There's only one way to find out, isn't there?"

We sat up until late, then I took him out into the garden after dark.

"Go on, get up that step-ladder."

"Why?"

He looked at me quizzically.

"Get up there and stretch your wings."

"Oh right. OK."

It wasn't one of the new, lightweight stepladders, but the one I had used for wallpapering. A solid, wooden affair with bits of rope strung between the sides and a couple of wicked hinges. I'd dragged it out of the shed earlier that day and set it up in the middle of the garden.

"I don't how you ever used one of these things," he grumbled, gingerly climbing the rungs with his naked feet.

"Ow! I've got a splinter."

He sucked his thumb.

"Don't be such a baby. Anyway, I didn't think you were supposed to feel such things."

"No, well. It's more the thought of it than anything else. My memories of mortal life are still very strong. Phantom pain, that's what they call it."

"Who are they?"

"The elders. The ones who teach us to fly."

"Well yours didn't do a very good job, did he?"

"She," he corrected.

"Hmmph. Woman driver. Might've known."

"Actually, you might know her."

Sitting on the top step of the ladder, he leaned forward and winked mischievously.

"Aggie?"

"I couldn't say ... I mean ... it's not allowed."

"But, I need to know. Please."

My throat thickened; then a torrent of hot tears ran down my cheeks.

"Please."

"Sorry, Fred. It's forbidden. We can't bring messages."

It wasn't manly – I'd never done it before – but I began to sob. Even at her grave, I'd been dry-eyed. Somehow, it had all gone inwards. A dry, desiccating sorrow that had sapped me of the will to live.

The dog next door began to howl.

"Come on, old man. Dry your eyes."

His hand was on my shoulder and I found myself enfolded in the feathery whiteness of his wings.

Then he cradled me in his arms, his cheek next to mine: his skin, warm and smooth, as soft as that of a child.

"I'll tell you something," he whispered. "It was no mistake I landed in your garden."

I pulled my face away and stared at him: my mouth sagging open; my nose, red and swollen, resembling that of a cartoon reindeer.

"I might be clumsy," he said. "But I'm not that bad. I was pushed."

I chuckled. Just like her. Then I wept while he held me, until all the pain had drained away.

"Fancy a trip," he said.

"What do you mean?"

"You could do with a change of scenery."

I could feel the muscles flex in his shoulders, then with a silky rustle, the great wings expanded.

"Wait a minute ..."

"Hang on tight."

There was a swooping sound, the sort made by swans as they fly overhead and suddenly we were airborne.

By this time, next door's dog was going mental: leaping at the fence and slavering at the mouth.

"What's the matter, Tobin?"

bit reminisce of the Snowman

I saw light pour onto their lawn as the neighbours opened the door. They both ran out, the girl in a short nightie and the man in track-suit bottoms.

"What is it, boy?"

I watched as they hunted around the garden. But they never looked up. People never do.

"Look, that's my parents' house."

Joey circled overhead. I could feel the longing in his heart. A swift stab of pain. But then we were off, rising higher and higher, soaring through an atmosphere sparkling with particles of ice: the land below a dark, black hulk, illuminated by dots and dashes of brilliance; a flickering code of street lamps and house lights.

"Where are we going?"

"You'll see."

The air became thinner as we continued to climb. My breath came in short, rasping gasps. I began to panic.

"Joey," I croaked. "Joey ..."

"Don't worry. We're nearly there."

He paused for a few seconds and we rotated slowly as he got his bearings. Then, without warning, he dived down. We were plummeting headlong through the sky and the nebulous mass that had been the earth acquired a sudden and terrifying substance as we hurtled towards it.

"Joey, Joey ...," I pleaded, but my voice was lost in the whistling slipstream.

I closed my eyes. *At least*, I thought, *it will be quick.*

I was still wondering whether it would be possible to feel excruciating pain for a nanosecond before death, when he suddenly pulled up short and I felt myself being gently lowered onto what felt like a cold, metal bench.

"You can open your eyes now."

Opening my eyelids a crack, I squinted out. The first thing I saw was my feet, then the ground, some fifty feet below.

"Ohh," I groaned, hiding my head in my hands.

"What's the matter?"

"I can't stand heights."

He roared with laughter.

"You're funny, you are. You've just been flying hundreds of feet above ground, no visible means of support and now, sitting on a nice firm bit of steel a few feet up, you're scared."

"I didn't have time to think before," I mumbled. "Anyway, where are we?"

"Where do you think?"

I squinted, trying to make out shapes in the darkness. I couldn't see much, but I could tell that the structure on which we sat was raised on a knoll. In the distance I could see a line of traffic. Beneath my hand, the metal felt rusty and when I turned my head to one side I could see a large, black shape like a human head.

"It's not ... It can't be ..." I stammered. "The Angel of the North?"

"Yep. That's right."

Joey swung his legs over the edge, looking pleased with himself.

"It's a good place to think. I've been here a couple of times already."

"Oh." I swallowed hard. The sight of my feet dangling below made me feel queasy.

"Look up," ordered Joey.

I did and instantly forgot my fear. Above me was a flickering gauze of green light; luminescent, and ethereal; a beauty that defied description, beyond the reckoning of art or poetry.

"That's the Northern Lights," said Joey, proudly.

"Aurora Borealis," I murmured.

"Eh?" said Joey, looking puzzled.

"Never mind."

We sat there until dawn. I must have slept because when I awoke, I was cradled in Joey's wings. He was humming to himself, hands resting on the Angel's metal wing, feet swinging over the edge.

Curled up in that downy hollow, it felt warm and safe. I had forgotten what it was like to be without fear; to sleep without nightmares or wake without the expectation of disaster.

Rubbing my eyes, I raised my head over the curve of his wing and saw the sky streaked with pink and the pale dome of the sun rising in the east.

I inspected my senses with newborn curiosity. Instead of sheltering from the cold – and it was gusty up there – I welcomed the wind on my face.

I revelled in colour and feasted on sound, unleashing my croaky, old man's voice in something resembling song.

Joey laughed and sang along, rocking me from side to side. Then, after a few minutes, he slipped his hands under my arms, linking his fingers over my chest.

"Time to be off," he said. "Next treat."

"Where?" I demanded, excitedly.

"A breath of fresh air."

We headed east towards the rising sun. The sky, an unblemished china blue, hinted at infinity. It was that magical time between the mystery of night and the obscurity of day when you can think and see with perfect clarity.

The air freshened. I could see sunlight glittering on water. The sea.

We took a sharp turn and headed north, swooping over beaches where a retreating tide had left ripples in the sand and a line of storm-wrecked weed marked the water's reach.

Diving low, we skimmed headlands and promontories, caught a fleeting reflection in rock-pools and circled the island where terns and puffins kept company with a white-washed light-house.

Then, turning in to the mainland, we dropped gently down to the beach.

Joey winked at me, mischievously.

"Remember this?"

Gently, he turned me round until I was facing a bank of dunes.

"Amble Links," I murmured. "It's where I used to come with Aggie."

He chuckled and put his arm around my shoulders. Strangely, I didn't feel sad: rather, invigorated, as if the life was flowing back into me, filling up the dark spaces that had lain empty for so long.

Little scenes of undervalued contentment began to play through my mind: bus-rides, sitting by the sea, eating iced buns from paper bags, watching birds feeding at the water's edge. All the things that I had forgotten to do since Aggie's death.

"Look!"

Joey was pointing excitedly at the sky. At first, I could see nothing: then a small fast-moving speck.

"Birds," I said.

"No. It's the Flight. They've come back for me. What shall I do?"

"Join them, of course."

"But I haven't time to get you back home. I can't leave you here."

"Yes, you can. And you must."

"But ..."

"Just go."

I gave him a shove in the back. He laughed.

"You're just like her, you know."

"I know. Now get on."

He spread his wings, put one foot behind the other like a runner and prepared to take off.

"There's just one thing ..."

"I know. I'll tell them."

"Thanks, Fred. I'll see you."

With one terrific bound, he leapt into the air, flying low at first, his wing tips skimming the foam. Then turning, he waved at me before soaring upwards and out of sight.

***

I was discovered by a couple of dog-walkers. They called the police, then an ambulance, then the social workers. I was rushed off to hospital, my vital signs checked, then given something to make me sleep.

I woke the next day in white, starchy sheets that were as tight as a straitjacket. A woman was sitting in a chair by the bed, a file perched on her knee. She was dressed in a plain, grey suit; cheap, unfussy, machine-washable; the sort worn every day as a kind of self-imposed uniform.

Her court shoes were nondescript, probably bought for comfort, and her hair was scraped back in a bun. The only startling thing about her was the sticky red gloss slicked over a humourless mouth.

"Hello, Mr Turner. I'm the hospital psychiatrist. I just want to ask a few questions."

Then she ran through the usual test. Who is the Prime Minister? Can you count to ten? What's the time? Where do you live?

I trotted out the answers and she raised an eyebrow as she ticked various boxes on her list.

"Good. Now. Can you tell me what you were doing on the beach?"

"I was going for a walk."

"In your carpet slippers and pyjamas?"

"Why not?"

That foxed her. She began to fiddle with her pen, clicking the button so that the nib popped in and out.

"Right. Well. How did you get there?"

"Bus."

"There's no bus at that time of morning. And you hadn't got a ticket. Or any money."

I didn't like the triumphant glint in her eye.

"Must've been the bus," I repeated.

"But there isn't one," she insisted.

"How else do you think I got there?" I asked.

She had no answer for that. She pursed her shiny red lips, clicked her pen and closed the file.

"We'll keep you in for another couple of days. Just

for observation. Then you can go home. This thing often happens after a bladder infection."

"A what?"

"It's quite common. Elderly people often lose their memory after a water infection. Nothing to worry about."

She rose to her feet, clamped her lips into a smile and clacked out of the room on her no-nonsense heels. Just outside, she was waylaid by one of the orderlies. By now, I'd become a bit of celebrity; even rated a couple of paragraphs in the local paper.

"Poor old sod," said the orderly. "They get like that when they get older. Confused. Like my uncle. They found him at the end of the pier – thought he was in France."

I didn't hear the psychiatrist's answer. But the brief pause in the clattering of her shoes implied that it was perfunctory.

***

I had a number of visitors in hospital, including Joey's parents. His father, Bob, was taciturn and angry, a typical expression of male grief; while his mother, Jenny, was red-eyed and voluble.

While Bob stood, looking out of the window, she

sat beside me, talking incessantly of nothing: as if, by filling the silence, she hoped to drive out the darker thoughts behind it.

After a few minutes, Bob muttered an excuse and lumbered out. He couldn't bear company, not even his own. As soon as he had gone, Jenny fell silent then, quietly, began to weep.

I took her hand and stroked it gently.

"He's all right, you know."

She leaned forward, staring deep into my eyes.

"Joey?" she murmured.

"You're not to worry. He's safe."

She bent forward and kissed me, just where Joey had kissed me, on the forehead.

She sat back, smiling, her fingers to her lips.

"You saw him, didn't you?"

I nodded.

"I knew about the accident. Long before they told me. I felt him, standing beside me. Just for a couple of seconds. But I made a mistake. I told Bob. He said I was mad."

"You're not."

I patted her hand.

She kissed me again and was gone.

***

When I got home, there were obligatory visits from the GP, social workers and health visitors. They all tried to persuade me to have 'carers' visit me in my home. I resisted with vigour. But in the end, just to appease them, I agreed to a twice-weekly visit from Brenda: a chubby girl with a workshy boyfriend and aspirations she could never fulfil.

On the first day, our conversation consisted of formalities. On the second, she told me her life story. On the third, she attempted to organise me.

"What's this?"

From across the room, she waved a large brown envelope filled with pieces of the vase that Joey had broken.

"It's a vase."

"A vase? You can't possibly mend it now. Smashed to bits. Shall I chuck it out?"

"No."

She placed it back on the shelf; no doubt planning to drop it in the bin when my back was turned.

"Look, you haven't even washed your windows. Look at all that dust. Funny how these things have a shape. I could swear it looked like a man. Why don't you let me clean it?"

"I'll get round to it. In my own time."

I must have spoken sharply because she looked downcast. She spent the rest of her time dusting, clucking over this and that, neatly stacking papers in no particular order. After she had gone, I phoned the agency and cancelled all future visits.

The next day, I woke before dawn. The house was quiet without Joey. I thought of his parents, especially Jenny, her eyes moist with grief. And I thought of Aggie.

Perhaps that outing in the cold air had weakened me. Perhaps I had imagined it after all. Was the psychiatrist right? Had I just suffered from loss of memory? The old feeling of dull hopelessness returned.

Dawn was creeping over the horizon as I hauled myself out of bed. My feet and legs felt leaden and my head ached: an after-effect of my trip to the sea.

How had I got there?

As I shuffled into the lounge, the first rays of sun lit up the outline of a man on the window: a man with wings. I sensed something different about the room.

Something on the table caught my eye.

There was the vase; complete, faultless. And, beside it, a pure white feather.

Not sure about ending.

Jack

The Treasure: The Green Man

In common with many religious buildings, Rochester Cathedral has a liberal sprinkling of Green Men. Their tiny faces peep out from the canopy of Bishop Hamo's tomb which is located by the Pilgrims' Steps in the North Quire Aisle while larger, brightly-painted versions peer down from the Crossing ceiling. Their appeal is timeless and they have been celebrated by both medieval masons and Victorian architects like Lewis Cottingham who worked on Rochester Cathedral from 1825 – 1840.

The origins of the Green Man are obscure. It has been claimed that versions of these foliate heads can be found in countries as far-flung as Borneo and Iraq and that some can be traced back to the 2nd century. Although initially associated with spring and fertility, the Green Man quickly found a new role within the Christian context, symbolising rebirth and resurrection. Rochester Cathedral has some 25 Green Men.

Closely allied to the Green Man is Jack-in-the-Green who appears in many English May Day celebrations including Rochester's Sweeps' Festival. Accompanied by Morris dancers, this character wears an all-encompassing metal framework covered in flowers and foliage.

My tale of *Jack* draws on Rochester's various associations with the Green Man. But it also relates to someone I met in childhood. Dressed entirely in green and pushing a handcart, a loveable but mysterious little man used to visit my mother's shop every spring. We never knew his name but I dedicate this story to his memory.

Jack

As spring slips through winter's fingers, you'll see Jack trundling his handcart along the Pilgrims' Way. Slowly, he weaves through narrow lanes, past high banks and hedges, always in pursuit of that other Jack; the cold cruel brother whose work he delights in undoing.

Ice cracks beneath his feet and buds fatten at his passing, turning black and spiny palisades into fruitful hedges. Trudging across the greening fields, he re-visits the woods of his youth where he takes his rest, leaning against a tree as he knits furiously with long needles that look, for all the world, like two smooth twigs.

The yarn is moss green and, as it slips between his gnarled fingers, the single skein loops and multiplies, purling itself into clothes: a balaclava, fingerless mittens, thick socks. His suit is made of different stuff, the colour of lichen; a jacket and short trousers reaching only to the knee. For, although he hates the cold, Jack likes to feel the keen bite of air on his skin.

He washes where he can, for Jack is always clean. Although village pumps have disappeared, he can still find water; dribbling from stand-pipes, trickling through streams, rising from forgotten springs where pilgrims filled their leather bottles. Sometimes, in the company of cattle, he bathes in ancient dew-ponds, laughing and splashing, scaring the birds – and occasional hikers.

Sprouting from his head and chin is a thick confusion of hair which, in defiance of age, changes rapidly from white to brown. Some accuse him of dying it. But Jack puts it down to exercise and a healthy life-style.

When hungry, he feasts on hawthorn buds, fresh from the twig. Squeezing them between thumb and forefinger, he rolls them into a ball before popping them in his mouth. What was it the children used to call them?

"A little bit of bread and no cheese," shrills the yellowhammer.

"No", says Jack. "A little bit of bread AND cheese. That's it."

Parting branches, he peeps into nests, smiling at mother birds who, with heads tilted to one side, fix him with bright enquiring eyes. Feeling beneath their quivering breasts, he counts the eggs, but never steals them. And, when he finds a naked nestling fallen from its refuge, he lifts it tenderly, cradling its pink nothingness in his brown hands, warming it with his breath, before returning it to the nest.

His progress is often slow for the cold makes his limbs creak. Sometimes he cannot move at all and hides himself beneath beds of leaves in woods and ditches where, in the dark, he examines the curling sprouts of ferns and speaks softly to seeds frozen in the earth. With his hand flattened to the ground, he feels the tingling of life in the cold, hard soil.

Across the Downs he trundles his cart, along narrow lanes and muddy tracks not made for cars where, despite the flare of night-lit towns, the woods are steeped in darkness. Beyond the open fields, black ridges of trees retain their timeless magic. Even now, few venture here at night, cowed by a nameless fear.

But Jack feels safe. Wrapped in his green tarpaulin, he stares through trees at the black-veined sky, and counts the constellations: Orion, Cassiopeia, Perseus. The motion of planets stirs his blood and, at full moon, he dances to their music; a sweet harmonious hum, like spinning tops.

By day, he meets the gypsies. A few still remember the old ways: fashioning baskets from switches of willow; filling them with primroses prised from the verge. Like Jack, they have no reckoning of rules or regulations, no sense of the new order that seeks to tether nomads and stop their wandering.

Yet, for all his love of the country, Jack does not despise the town. For here he is remembered: by artists and architects, stonemasons and storytellers. And always he is drawn to one place by the sweet singing of voices and the faces of his brethren.

Stepping back through history, he follows a winding route: past Stone Age barrows and the ford where Romans fought embattled Britons; past the grave of a sailor who held the dying Nelson in his arms; on to the river whose wide span runs with fire in the setting sun.

Yet even here, where rising tides carry the salt smack of the sea, winter lingers. And there is more work for Jack.

At night, his breath melts frost from glass, warming the cold frames. Through bedroom windows, he spies gardeners dreaming of delicious dahlias and, for their delight, he slips into potting sheds and wakes the rude tubers slumbering in crates of earth, tickling them with his soil-stained fingers.

On his way to the City, Jack parks his handcart outside a little shop and, taking a seat inside, places his order: six balls of wool, moss green.

"Double-knit or four-ply?" asks the woman at the counter. "Or something with a nice bit of cashmere?"

Every year, the same rigmarole. Jack pretends to choose while the woman brings him tea and biscuits. They discuss the weather and, as usual, she reveals her life to him, while he says nothing of his. She will never know where he comes from, or where he goes. But each year, she waits for his return and is never disappointed.

Old Jack can keep a secret, so she tells him all her hopes and fears, the pain that has crept into her joints. Tale upon tale tumbles out – births, deaths and marriages – in no particular order.

Meanwhile, Jack crunches through digestives and hobnobs, dunking ginger nuts in his tea and catching the soggy end in his mouth just before it peels off and splashes in the cup.

"Same as usual," he says, wiping the crumbs from his beard.

"I'm sorry?"

The woman is caught mid-flow; some scandal about a neighbour's wife and the coal merchant.

"Same as usual," says Jack, placing four shining coins on the counter.

"Oh, of course."

The woman wraps the balls of wool in a brown

paper bag and, neatly folding the end, seals it with sellotape.

"Thank you."

Ever the gentleman, Jack executes a little bow and pulls open the shop door which sets a wind-chime tinkling. He pauses, thoughtful, as if reminded of something he had forgotten.

"Remember to prune that apple tree in your garden."

Before she can thank him, he is gone.

"Well how did he know that?" she murmurs.

Yet, for all his strangeness, she is reassured. Tonight, she will sleep better than she has for weeks, drifting off to the sound of the shipping forecast with a seed catalogue lying open beside her. New beginnings.

Dragging his cart up the steep road from the river, Jack passes the ruined castle and stops to catch his breath, perching on a low wall under the bare branches of the Catalpa tree. An exotic introduction from the New World, the tree flourishes in many churchyards, although no-one can remember precisely who planted this one, or when. Like Jack, its origins are a mystery.

Parking his cart in an angle of the wall, Jack enters the Cathedral, passing through the Norman arch flanked by statues of the builder-bishop who, like the Catalpa tree, left his native country to thrive on foreign soil. Only he laid seeds of stone that grew into a Cathedral, a castle and London's bloody Tower.

Face shining, Jack trots along the Nave, heading for the Pilgrims' Steps. But it is not a shrine that he seeks; no casket of saintly bones, but the image of his brothers. He finds them, hiding in the stone canopy of a bishop's tomb. As he strokes their faces, the stone leaves running from their mouths turn green, quiver and flourish, shooting out tendrils that wind around his fingers.

He chuckles then, putting a finger to his mouth, says "Hush!" The leafy sprouts sink back into the stone, the faces lose their colour; but each seems to smile a little wider, their eyes crinkling at the corners, in homage to Jack.

"I must go and find the others," he whispers.

He makes his way to the Crossing where, high in the tower is a brightly painted ceiling: the folly of a Victorian architect. Guarding a trap-door to the belfry, are four of Jack's brethren: a gallery of rough brown men with startled eyes and tombstone teeth, foliage trailing from their mouths. One has a broken nose and looks as if he spent his life at sea, brawling in hostelries and swabbing decks until, one day, he stumbled into this place of peace.

Jack cranes his neck, squinting into the darkness overhead. There is only one way to get a better view. He takes off his green jacket and carefully rolls it into a bolster.

Across the way is a little shop, selling guide-books, rosaries, leather book-marks and postcards.

"Look!" says the young assistant. "There's another one taking photographs."

But his colleague shakes her head.

"No," she says. "That's just Jack. He comes at this time every year. Always spends a few minutes like that, staring at the ceiling."

Hands behind his head, Jack rests on the cold stone, his pilgrimage finished. Wearied by travelling, he can no longer fight sleep. His eyelids flicker. Outside, daffodils shoot through the trembling soil to point their spikes at heaven.

The Wheel of Fortune

The Treasure: The Wheel of Fortune wall painting

The Wheel of Fortune or *Rota Fortunae* dates back to classical times. A popular motif in medieval art, it portrayed Fortune as a woman – often wearing a crown – turning a huge wheel. As the wheel turned, small figures would be shown rising on one side of it while falling off the other. A richly-clad king would often sit astride the wheel while, directly beneath him, a beggar would be shown, crushed under the wheel's weight.

While many of the medieval depictions of the Wheel of Fortune are found in illuminated manuscripts, the version at Rochester Cathedral is painted on the wall of the Quire. Ironically, only the portion of the painting depicting good fortune remains. It was discovered behind a pulpit in the 19th century: a hiding place which protected it from whoever destroyed the section portraying bad luck. The likely culprits were Cromwell's soldiers who used the Cathedral to stable their horses.

I was struck by the irony that Fortune herself survived due to good luck. This inspired the first story in this section, entitled 'Lady Luck'.

Regnabo, regno, regnavi, sum sine regno. This Latin saying describes the turn of the Wheel and the changing fortunes of those carried along by it. Translated, it means: I shall reign, I reign, I have reigned, I have no realm. It seemed appropriate to allow Fortune herself to repeat these words as a kind of chorus.

The second story 'A Turn around the Supermarket' was partly based on observations taken from life. Even in a mundane context, it is possible to see the proud being humbled. The Wheel of Fortune is a reminder that life can change dramatically at any moment.

Part I - Lady Luck

I am Fortune's time-keeper; the unseen cog in human affairs; the counterweight of ambition. My wheel turns steadily, raising poor men to riches, unseating the powerful, reducing them to dust. I am a pagan in a holy place; daughter of an ancient world. But my message endures. Fate is fickle.

As I turn my wheel, men rise and fall. The lowly servant, trapped beneath his master's heel, clutches at his lord's garment, hoping for betterment; the master, richly-dressed yet discontented, plots his rise to power; the king, seated on his throne, keeps a wary eye on those who would take it from him.

The Wheel turns once more. The former ruler slips from glory; the man whom Fortune has abandoned, hurtles earthwards to become the lowest of men.

Regnabo, regno, regnavi, sum sine regno.

From my sanctuary, I have seen them all: proud kings and bishops, nobles and martyrs. I have witnessed rebels shout defiance from the Castle walls. I have let them strut the battlements and savour freedom before delivering them into a tyrant's hands.

I clapped when Cromwell's soldiers turned God's house into a stable and I cheered with the crowds when the king returned. *Hoorah for jolly King Charles, dancing and debauchery*. I cheered again when his brother, King James, was banished.

A benighted age tried to wipe me from its memory, scraping half my portrait from the walls. But, by a stroke of Fate, I survived; along with that part of my Wheel that raises men to power. You could call it Good Fortune.

The Victorians ignored my lessons. Old wisdom was treated with contempt. The arc of Fate was hammered out of shape: flattened, flat-lined and filled with linear purpose. Converted by zealous hands, it became a one-way track to glory. No returns.

Like ancient Romans, these 19th century conquerors decked their temples with trophies, reckless of their power or meaning. Pagan symbols, bereft of potency, were jumbled together: fragments of a dead language; its tongue silent, its alphabet askew. Sacred space became a cornucopia: crammed with mementos that spoke, not of death, but of ambition.

Destiny became the slave of men. Nations were claimed then trussed with iron. Roads, railways, canals, steam-engines and aquifers. They raised an Empire. And then it fell. With a little help from me.

Regnabo, regno, regnavi, sum sine regno.

Arrogance will be punished.

Yet, for all the mistreatment I have suffered at the hands of mortals, I still have favourites. Not the ones you would expect. But those who accept Fate as part of life. They appreciate its ironies. Just as I do. Here is one of them now. A journalist taking her lunch-break. And she has a story to tell.

Part II - A Turn around the Supermarket

Ivisit the Cathedral most days. For a walk and a bit of peace. In the summer, I eat my sandwiches sitting on the wall outside: watching people, making mental sketches of the interesting ones; for the novel I plan to write.

I've got an idea for the plot. A really good one. But I need time. I keep meaning to start but there are always distractions; work, children, the garden, the house, the car. Somebody always needs my attention; something always diverts me from my goal.

So that's why I come here. Every lunch-hour, seeking refuge, I step into the Cathedral's cool, dark space and become weightless, unencumbered.

Upon the grey flagstones, I release my thoughts, letting them soar among the vaults and arches, waiting for them to settle. They return quietly; no longer a fluttering chaos, but an arrow-shaped phalanx; each following the other in orderly flight.

Sometimes, I find a quiet corner and write some lines for my novel. Or I walk, slowly, without purpose, letting the Cathedral guide me. Everywhere, I hear the whisper of voices: a Babel without clangour. I am surrounded, but not pursued: visible yet unseen.

I watch and listen, sharp as a hunter, my senses honed. Inspiration lies around the corner: curled up in corners, hiding in faces, hovering over tombs, awaiting discovery. Today, it is the Wheel of Fortune. Or what remains of it.

Sleeping behind a pulpit, this Lady Luck defied the ravages of war and kept her royal crown. Not so the unfortunates whose luck descended with her wheel. Condemned to obscurity, their fate was sealed by Cromwell's soldiers who scraped them from the walls. Not a scrap of paint records their sad faces or struggling limbs. A turn of the Wheel sent them to oblivion.

This painting of Lady Luck, with her blush-pink cheeks and golden hair, reminds me of a woman in the supermarket this morning. A mother with upward aspirations, ready to climb, push and scramble up the Wheel of Fortune, heedless of others crushed under its weight.

A catalogue-fresh 'yummy-mummy', dressed in 'prep-school' style: blonde hair tucked behind an Alice-band, padded gilet, kilt, thick knitted tights and sensible nubuck boots: a she-wolf in lamb's clothing.

I first encountered her by the exotic vegetables. She had placed a single aubergine on the scales. No plastic bag. Having dabbed at the instructions, she looked around vacantly, slowly turning her head from side to side. I was two feet away, but she was as unaware of me as an ostrich in the Kalahari. Finally, she surrendered; dropping the aubergine – unwrapped – into her trolley.

Leave it to the woman at the cash-desk. It's what she's paid for.

It was half-term and she was accompanied by two children: hers, presumably, because they called her *Mummy*. Although, when they spoke, she looked bemused, as if she didn't recognise them.

While upwardly mobile, her progress around the store was slow. Parked by the organic pasta and cannellini beans, with her phone plugged into her ear, she dictated instructions, loud and slow; exercising remote control.

Meanwhile, her children – Bella and Tarquin – pursued a campaign of terror. Urban commandos, practised in the art of skid and crash, they tormented the shoppers and worried the shelves. Racing around the aisles, they shrieked to a halt, plunging their arms into chiller-cabinets to pester the peas and molest the mange-touts, before dashing off to stir up the porridge and rattle the cornflakes.

Blissfully ignorant, with one aubergine in her trolley, Mother continued to give orders over the phone.

A shout of *Pizza, Pizza* as the children swooped on the Ready Meals.

Mother unplugged the phone from her ear.

A murmured discussion, followed by an altercation, ending with a plea of: "Why not?"

Mother shook her head and glided on.

Disappointed, Bella and Tarquin raced off to harry the shelves, re-arranging some unsuspecting beans and canned ratatouille before their mother caught up.

"What's this?" demanded Tarquin, waving a packet of cut-price pasta over his head.

Mother bent over, inspected the label and nodding her head, permitted him to drop it into the trolley.

"At last," bellowed Tarquin. "Something we can afford."

Mother plugged her phone back into her ear, quickly arranging her features in a look of blank insouciance. But I saw her wince and was glad.

In the hope of avoiding them, I made my way to the cafe. Too late. They had got there before me. Mother was at the counter, brandishing a voucher that entitled her to free coffee.

"A latte, please."

"I want a croissant, Mummy", demanded Tarquin.

"A croissant?" she murmured, eyes registering alarm.

The assistant beamed.

"Can I help?"

Cornered, Mother looked plaintively at the woman behind the counter.

"Do you have a croissant?"

It was a rhetorical question, requiring a single answer: *No*.

But, armed with tongs and a large white plate, the assistant hunted up and down the counter. Diligently, she lifted lids, searched in cupboards and even disappeared into the store-room.

There was an audible sigh of relief when she declared that they were '*out of croissants*'.

Mother then congratulated the assistant on the perfection of her latte, admiring the little white saucer with a button-sized biscuit that accompanied it.

"Could I buy another one of those?" she enquired.

Pointing at the biscuit, she cracked open her designer purse: hinting at payment, without intent.

"That's all right, dear. I'll give you *two*", crooned the assistant. "I don't usually but who could look at those little faces and resist?"

Two pairs of round, moon-like eyes had risen over the counter-top and were fixed, not on the button-sized biscuits, but on a pile of pastries smothered in icing.

With a smile like confectioners' cream, Mother thanked the assistant and, penning the children into a corner table, settled down to her coffee with an expression of quiet triumph.

At the check-out, they appeared again. Right in front of me. Just my luck!

Tarquin was complaining loudly about some extra-curricular lessons. Mother countered with her own brand of logic.

"Darling, if you don't do your work, you won't get to a good school. And if you don't do that, you won't get a good job. You'll end up working in a place like this. Just like the lady at this till."

The girl at the till registered no emotion.

As the aubergine and the pasta sailed along the conveyor belt, a fight broke out.

"Ow! Bella you pinched me."

"Ooh. Bella. That's a pretty name," cooed the cashier. "Are you a fan of the Twilight Saga?"

"What?" retorted Mother, angrily.

"It's a story about vampires," offered the cashier, innocently.

Mother feigned disgust.

"Certainly not!"

Gathering the children to her, she exited with as much dignity as her lightly-laden trolley would allow, hurrying to the disabled bay where she had parked her 4x4. Without a blue badge.

"No," mused the cashier, gazing after the woman. "Twilight Saga's not her kind of book. More like 50 Shades of Grey."

She winked at me.

"Actually," she said, helping me to stuff my bread rolls into a plastic bag, "this is my holiday job. I'm studying French at Cambridge."

The Baker's Boy

The Treasure: William of Perth

The story of William of Perth is a medieval mystery. How did an obscure pilgrim from Scotland become the patron saint of Rochester?

What little is known of William's life is recounted by the *Nova Legenda Anglie.* He was reputed to be a baker from Perth, a wild youth who became a devout Christian and dedicated every tenth loaf to the poor.

While William's pilgrimage to England from Scotland reflects the religious culture of the time, his progression from anonymity to sainthood is less easy to explain. To do this, his life needs to be viewed within a wider historical context (see Appendix).

In the years prior to William's death, the devastating effects of two fires and the imposition of a new papal tax would have placed a heavy burden on the religious community at Rochester.

The creation of Canterbury's contemporary saint – Thomas Becket – may have suggested a solution. William of Perth's death could well have provided an opportunity to emulate Canterbury's success.

The account of William's life was added to the *Legenda* over three centuries after his death and cannot be substantiated. For that reason, I have used a writer's licence and departed from some of the details recorded in that source.

We shall probably never know the true facts about William's life – or his death. My story is based on surmise: one version of what *might* have been.

What is beyond dispute is that William's shrine provided a substantial source of income. At a critical point in the Cathedral's fortunes, William played an important part in preserving this beautiful building for future generations. For this reason, he deserves a place among its treasures.

The Baker's Boy

I was found on the doorstep. A squalling infant, cheeks pinched with cold; the filthy rag in which I was wrapped freckled with the first flakes of snow.

A gift from God: or so he said. For by adopting me, he won the praise of Perth, our home town. I was another token of his generosity. William, the baker, who gave every tenth loaf to the poor. William who attended Mass every day and spent so much time on his knees that many wondered how he ever managed to stoke the ovens.

No such renown for me. I was David the Foundling: *Cockermay Doucri* in the old Scots tongue. A child regarded as fortunate for having been abandoned at William's door. No matter that I was unwanted and unloved. No matter that the town never knew the truth. I was the lightening rod for God's grace; a mirror whose only purpose was to reflect William's glory.

But I knew different.

It was William's wife who was the saint. A pale, sickly girl who spat blood when she coughed and whose body, racked with pain, bore the marks of many beatings; although William made sure that her bruises were concealed by fine, warm clothes. She, too, was the victim of his outward generosity.

It was she who took me in.

One night, slipping from William's hot embrace, she left him snoring in their narrow bed and tip-toed down the stairs to the kitchen, hoping to stifle her cough with a drink of small beer. As she warmed her hands over the low embers of the fire, she heard a mewling at the door.

Not a cat. At least, not hers; for that was curled up on the hearth.

She crept across the room, the rushes that strewed the floor crackling under her naked feet. Sliding back the iron bar, she opened the door a crack and peeped out. A gust of wind smote her eye. She blinked, a bitter tear rolling down her cheek.

Peering once again into the dark alley, she saw first a whorl of snow, a celestial brightness suspended above the noisome cobbles. Then, a puff of wind and streams of powdery ice flowed into the street from the close-knit roofs of houses.

Spellbound, she looked up and saw snowflakes racing towards her through the darkness and, although she stood still, she felt as if she were flying through space. Lifting up her arms to the sky, she let the snow caress her face with a gentleness never shown to her by human hands.

A murmur. She looked down and, with eyes now

accustomed to the darkness, saw a bundle stowed in the angle of the step. She bent to touch it and parting the rags, discovered the dead-white face of a baby.

Picking it up, she ran back into the house, leaving the print of her naked feet on the step.

Laying the tiny body by the fire, she threw more wood on the embers, chafed the tiny hands and, blowing into the cold mouth, revived the little creature with her own breath. Then, with a drop of warm milk on her finger, she placed it on the infant's tongue. The limbs flexed and a small hand clutched at her gown.

"Sweetheart," she murmured, as the dark eyes opened and fixed her in their gaze.

***

In the morning, he found them together, asleep under a blanket in front of the fire, she with the child clutched to her sparrow's breast.

For that, she got a beating. But when he threatened to turn the child out, she argued with him boldly, citing the damage to his reputation. No amount of alms-bread could blunt the shame of abandoning a baby.

Yet, if he wished to improve his standing with the

monks and the burghers, what better way to prove his generosity than to give this child a home? And, if she were unable to give him a son, they could raise this one as their own.

For the foundling was a boy; a welcome pair of hands to whom William could entrust his business. Far better than any apprentice who, having learned the trade, could take his skill elsewhere. What better way to provide for their old age?

And what better way to still the wagging tongues?

"What do you mean?" he bellowed, clenching his fist.

Her arms cradling her head, she peered up at him, cowed yet with a spark of cunning. She said nothing, but met his eyes, exchanging anger for intelligence. Unlike the townspeople, she was not blinded by his professions of faith.

She remembered all the stories that they had forgotten. Tales of William's wildness: his drinking, whoring and brutality. She knew that these were not youthful indiscretions. They had not disappeared or lessened with age. He had just learned to conceal them better.

Trembling, she reasoned with him. His rejection of the foundling child could lead to questions.

Who was the child's mother and why had she left him at William's door?

He raised his fist. She braced herself for the torrent of blows. But this time, they did not come.

"Keep the brat," he muttered as he strode out of the house, slamming the door behind him.

For five years, she nurtured me as if I was her own and, despite the beatings, we were happy.

But in the shrinking cold of another winter, disaster struck. Worn down by her illness and as frail as a reed, my mother finally succumbed to the cough that had plagued her for years.

At least, that is what William told me; although, on the night of her death, he had been drinking heavily. Quivering under my blanket, I heard everything: yells, curses, sharp slaps, the dull thud of fists. The next morning she was dead.

The earth was so hard that it had to be broken with a pick. I watched tearfully as my mother, wrapped in a winding sheet, was lowered into her grave. Burying his face in his fat hands, my father bawled heartily within earshot of the other mourners. Yet he spoke no word to me.

When we returned home, he sat morose and silent by the fire, staring into its molten heart. I watched dark thoughts play across his face in the flickering light until the last spark died, consigning us both to darkness.

From that day, I became both his slave and his guardian.

***

As I grew, he taught me his trade. Together we nurtured the mother dough on which our livelihood depended. The slow-growing yeast culture was many years old. It had to be watched and fed, nourished like a delicate invalid and kept warm; neither too hot, nor too cold. Summer's basting heat would kill it as surely as winter's stinging cold.

Every week, I accompanied William to market where, digging his hand into sacks of flour, he would let the powder trickle through his fingers then examine what remained in his palm.

After that, came the haggling. My father, his cheeks puffed out, would roar at the merchant. The merchant roared back and soon, it seemed, they would come to blows. Then, suddenly, it was over. The merchant and my father would shake hands, slap each other on the back and share a drink from a greasy, leather bottle.

After that, the merchant's boy would load the flour onto our cart and my father, by this time none too steady, would lead our small pony back through the narrow streets to the bakery where, after unloading the cart, he would fall asleep on top of the sacks.

Our flour was made from local barley, rye and wheat; poor quality grain contaminated with corncockle, fit only for the poor. For years, I made those dense dark loaves, kneading them with angry intensity as I imagined my father's puffy face beneath my knuckles. As I pummelled the dough, rough with impurities, I dreamed of revenge – or of running away.

Was it anger that fuelled my hatred? Or desperation? I cannot say. But being shackled to him was torture. I had pierced the veil of a man thought to be a saint, but who I knew to be a devil. I was the keeper of his secrets and the knowledge nearly sent me mad.

After my mother's death, my father's passion for prayer became a torment. Every day, it was Mass and Confession. Together, we knelt before the priest and begged forgiveness (although I had no notion of what sin I had committed). I watched William as he wept with exaltation and was forced to accompany him to the priory every day to deliver alms-bread for the poor.

Yet, as his outward observance of religion became more extreme, so did his private excess.

At night, we slept on the bakery floor, covered with flour sacks for warmth as we waited for the dough to prove. It was here that he brought his women and I lay with my fingers in my ears to block out the sound of their lewd coupling.

In the morning, he would force me down onto the cold stone floor and make me pray with him, muttering and moaning like a man beset by a succubus who struggles feebly in his sleep.

When the bread was baked, he would go to Confession, leaving me in charge of the shop: the only time he left my side. In the evening, he would take me to Benediction: more praying, more kneeling, more tears.

I was his companion in madness; a silent observer of a sick mind. My life was measured, not in seasons, but by the fermenting of yeast and the ringing of bells.

One evening in early spring, there was a knock at the door.

"Go and answer it!" growled my father.

We had been eating our supper by the fire: a flavourless potage; beans stewed with a few cubes of fatty mutton and a sprinkling of salt. I set my wooden bowl on the hearth, reluctant to leave the warmth.

Beyond the fire's meagre radiance, the room was cold and frost was creeping under the door.

Outside, the sky over the rooftops was streaked with gold, although night had already crept into the street. A dark figure was standing on the step. As my eyes became accustomed to the gloom, I saw it was a girl, not more than fifteen years old, a rough woollen cloak wrapped tightly about her.

"Who is it?" shouted my father.

"Tell him to come here!" said the girl, raising her voice as she peered over my shoulder.

"Tell him to come here and face me."

A chair scraped on the floor. My father shambled across the room and stood behind me, blinking.

"Who are you?" he demanded.

But there was fear in his voice.

"Don't you recognise me?" said the girl, her voice even louder. "Then perhaps you'll recognise this!"

She drew back her cloak to reveal her belly. Her time was near.

"My brothers have threatened to kill the man if they find him."

"No!"

My father was shaking, his face pasty and sagging.

"I don't know who you are!"

"No? You pursued me long enough. You forced me ..."

"I never did."

"... against my will. There's a law for that."

"It's not true."

But I knew that it was. More than any confession, his looks betrayed him. He was scarlet and his lips had a bluish tinge. Tearing at the neck of his shirt, he seemed to be struggling for air.

"Well! What is it to be?"

The girl persisted.

"Do I tell them who it was?"

"No, no!"

Lights were appearing behind shuttered windows. Along the street, a door opened.

"What's the noise?"

"Nothing neighbour," I shouted. "All's well."

The girl's eyes glittered in the dark. Bent on furious confrontation, she took a step towards my father. But his will to fight had gone. He gaped at her, unable to speak.

I took the girl's arm and led her indoors, offering her a seat by the fire.

"You must talk," I said. "You must decide together what to do."

"He could always marry me," she taunted.

My father trembled violently as if on the verge of a fit.

"But, of course, he'd never do that," she added.

"Why not?" I asked.

"She's a witch," murmured my father, his eyes wide with terror.

"Is it true?" I asked.

"If you mean "Do I share his religion?" then no, I do not."

"Pagan devil!" shouted my father. "You should be burnt for your sins."

"And what of yours?"

"I confess. I ask forgiveness."

"So you're free to sin again!"

The girl laughed loudly, throwing back her head. In the firelight, her hair and eyes gleamed black. Her skin, too, was unusually dark.

"You're a gypsy!" I murmured.

"Yes. And I have a fine family of men who will pull this house down around your father's ears ... after they have baked him in his own oven."

"Stop, stop. I will marry you," my father blethered in desperation.

"And who says I will have you?" laughed the girl.

"Then what is it you want?"

"Money," she said simply.

"How much?"

She named her price. He gasped.

"You have brought a child into the world," she reminded him. "It must be paid for. And we gypsies love gold."

"But I do not have that sum," he pleaded.

"Find it!" she hissed. "Or I will denounce you to the town. I will not leave *my* child on your doorstep."

Rising from her chair, she briefly held my gaze, regarding me with pity. Then she turned to my father.

"I will be back tomorrow for your answer."

She spat the words at him.

My father slumped heavily into a chair, his face blank and uncomprehending. The girl regarded him disdainfully, then gathering her cloak about her, she turned to leave.

As she passed me, she murmured: "You are no foundling."

As the door slammed behind her, my father was seized by a fit of rage: the dying throes of a baited bear when the dog's jaws close around its throat. Jumping to his feet, he grabbed the heavy club that we kept by the hearth and headed for the door.

"I'll kill her. The grasping whore! No-one will

question it. Who'll care about the body of gypsy girl lying in a ditch? I'll beat her brains out."

"You'll do no such thing!"

I flung myself at him, gripping him by the shoulders then, realising that I would be unable to restrain him otherwise, I dealt him several fierce blows to the face, pounding his doughy flesh with my knuckles. He gasped and staggered, clutching his hand to his nose, blood trickling between his fingers; then, white and shaking, he fell back onto his chair.

That night, I sat with him for many hours. At first, he could not speak and I thought that he had fallen into a fit. His face distorted by firelight resembled that of a carved curiosity. I had seen them often, staring down at me from the ceiling of the church: not the elegant faces of bishops and nobles that adorned the tombs, but the swollen, ugly faces of townspeople, fingers pulling down the corners of their mouths, heads bound in rags, groaning with toothache; lustful monks and peasants who, from their elevated position, ogled the burghers' wives passing below. A mason's joke.

"Who am I?" I asked, finally.

In a voice, barely audible, he whispered: "A mistake."

Seized with rage, I clenched my fists, resisting the urge to hit him again.

"Why did you not acknowledge me?"

"I was married. You were born out of wedlock. I could not stand the shame."

"The shame?" I yelled.

Unable to look at me, he murmured: "My reputation. I had a reputation."

"What reputation?" I shouted. "A few mouldy loaves for the poor every week? What sort of reputation is that, compared to abandoning your own child?"

Slowly, he raised his eyes to my face and, in them, I read the answer. I had been his shame. A child begotten who knows where or with whom. A child that he had tried to reject.

But his wife had not let him. Clever woman that she was, she had forced him to confront his sin. Every day, when he looked at me, he remembered. But it had not cured him. It had only increased his malice and anger, resulting in even greater depravity.

And now there was another child. But this time, it would not be a foundling. I would make sure of that.

"You must sell the bakery. Give that gypsy girl what she asks."

"But ..."

Bleary-eyed, he gazed at me, silently pleading, hoping to change my mind. Anger surged within me. I would strike down whatever excuse he made.

"... I was keeping it for you. The bakery is for you. It's your birthright."

It was not the answer I had expected. I stared deep into his bloodshot eyes. For the first time, they revealed a spark of misshapen love. I wanted to howl. All this time and never a kind word. Now this. And what had prompted him to admit his feelings? Another woman that he had wronged!

I lowered my head, so that he could not see my face, or the angry tears coursing down my cheeks.

"It is no longer my birthright," I snarled. "You have two children now."

"But what will we do without the bakery?"

He had never asked my opinion before.

"We'll go away."

"Away? But where?"

"Pilgrimage."

How did that word find its way to my lips? It had not been in my thoughts.

"Pilgrimage?"

"Yes. With the cold biting your limbs and sores plaguing your feet, you will pay for what you have done. I will see that you do."

"You will come with me, then?"

It was a request, humbly made; not an assumption. Without its usual note of arrogance, his voice sounded weak and uncertain.

"Yes," I replied, somewhat quelled. "We will visit the holy places together."

Together. A word that breached his loneliness; a chink of light shining into the prison of his soul.

He held his hand out to me. But I did not take it. Instead, I sat quietly, forcing him to speak by my silence. I listened as he confessed: his love for a young and beautiful woman; his joy at their marriage; his rage at her sickness.

The fear of losing her had stalked him, both waking

and sleeping. Seeking oblivion, he had worked like a demon, stoking the ovens, bound to their infernal heat, feeding the yeast, pounding the dough.

And when there was not enough work, he had lost himself in drunkenness and lust. His wife knew all and forgave him. But her goodness drove him to fury and he beat her without mercy. That last night, her heart as fragile as a bird's, had fluttered and stopped.

"God forgive me," he wept, pressing his knuckles into his eyes.

"He still may. All who repent will be forgiven."

I do not know where the words came from. Perhaps I had heard them from a priest. I had always dismissed such talk as empty mumbling: Pardoners' puff; the talk of men who put a price on forgiveness. But now it had meaning.

***

There was no shortage of buyers for the bakery. Soon, everything was sold; flour, kindling, kneading troughs; even the mother dough that we had tended for so long. As the money changed hands, others moved in to stoke the ovens and bake the bread.

Having provided for the gypsy girl and her child, my father cast off his old life. To mark this change, he assumed the traditional garb of a pilgrim: a staff, a satchel and a long tunic of coarse woollen cloth called a sclavein. As for me, I kept my old clothes.

For many months, we trudged the highways in wind, rain, sun and snow, our feet bleeding and blistered, our fingers blighted with chilblains. Gradually, I noticed a change in my father: small acts of kindness and a growing ability to endure hardship and deny himself pleasure.

If food ran short, he would give me what remained. If we were caught in a storm, he would find me a dry spot in which to shelter, even if there was no place for him. He would watch over me while I rested, patiently enduring sleet and snow, drenched to the skin, water dripping from the hem of his sclavein which, in cold weather, would freeze into a blade of ice that ripped his skin.

With bitter pain, he strove to become a good father. Yet, though he sought to win my love, I could not give it. For my anger still ran hot. Present kindness could not erase the memory of past cruelty. My heart remained knot-hard.

Sometimes, I caught him looking at me sadly and I turned away. I would not forgive him. Not yet. He must pay for all he had done. If I heard him weeping quietly at night – as he often did – I would stop my ears. I would not be swayed. He must earn his redemption.

***

We travelled south, following a route that would eventually bring us to the shrine of St Thomas at Canterbury. On the way, we prayed at many shrines: some famous, such as those of St Cuthbert at Durham and Our Lady at Walsingham; others, known only to local people, which we discovered along the way.

In towns, we would stay in inns or guest-houses run by the monastic orders. In the country, we would have to shift for ourselves, sleeping warm in hay-barns or cold on cottage floors.

Occasionally, we lost our way and stranded far from habitation, we hid behind hedges and crouched in ditches, spending a sleepless night until daybreak, praying that the evil spirits that stalked lonely places would not find us.

In our wanderings, we met other pilgrims with whom we often travelled for safety; for deserted country roads and woodland tracks were the domain of robbers and outlaws. Even in daylight, you could hear their soft footfall behind hedges or see their fleeting shadows between the trees as they stalked their prey.

***

Some forty miles from Canterbury, we broke our journey at Rochester. The City, lapped by the wide waters of the Medway, had a fine cathedral. Within its precincts, the Benedictine priory of St Andrew offered hospitality to pilgrims.

The guest-house was simple and the food, plain. But after a long day's journey it offered shelter and a respite from danger and discomfort. After taking their meal in the refectory, pilgrims would gather together in groups, sharing tales of their life on the road.

I fell into conversation with a blacksmith called John. He wore a scallop shell, drilled with two small holes and sewn onto his hat, the token of St James whose shrine he had visited in Spain.

He was a big man with broad shoulders and forearms as thick as a leg of mutton. Yet despite his physical strength, John had a commonsense approach to the road and a stern warning for fellow wayfarers.

"Never travel alone, lad," he said, clapping me on the back.

I marvelled at this strong man's caution. He laughed.

"Not even I could withstand a band of ten or twenty men. I suppose you can't blame them. They have little to live on except thieving. Pilgrims wandering about unprotected with money in their scrips must be a sore temptation."

"You pity them?"

"Our Lord died in the company of thieves. He even promised Paradise to one of them. You can't always judge a man by his circumstances," he said, thoughtfully.

I nodded meekly. We fell into thoughtful silence; then, grinning, John prodded me in the chest with his forefinger.

"And don't trust everyone you meet, even if they're pilgrims – or appear to be. You'll find as many rogues at shrines as you will in the open country. Wolves to whom pilgrims are no more than bleating sheep, ready for slaughter."

He wished me goodnight, leaving me to ponder his words.

A group of pilgrims had gathered by the fire, my father among them. Although much changed, he had not lost his craving for admiration. He still had a tendency to brag and was recounting how much he had earned from the sale of his bakery. His boastfulness always piqued me; but tonight, with

John's warning fresh in my mind, fear increased my anger.

Most of the company appeared drowsy or bored: all except two men. They had drifted in from the edge of the group and were standing in an angle of the fire-place where, partially concealed in shadow, they were listening attentively to my father.

A log in the hearth crackled and threw up sparks, illuminating the face of one of the men. He had lean, vulpine features, the sort that sniff out weakness; Reynard the Fox in human form. His lips were drawn back in a thin, hungry smile.

I hurried over to my father and, hooking my arm through his, urged him to come to bed. He muttered angrily but, to my relief, allowed himself to be led away. At the door, I looked over my shoulder and caught the man glowering at me; a fox robbed of its quarry.

***

We rose before dawn to attend Prime. The harmony of monkish voices enfolded us, swelling, surging, welling over the cold stone, spilling into every corner before disappearing into the infinite darkness above. And suddenly there was light: red, yellow and blue; dancing over capitals and pillars; jewels flung from stained glass windows, released by the rising sun.

For an instant, my heart knew heaven.

Yet our peace was short-lived. The masons were already at work, their hammering and shouting battling with the plainsong, their coarse voices challenging its purity.

After the service, we took a light breakfast of bread and ale. After that, I left my father with the other pilgrims while I took a last look at the Cathedral. In the cloisters, I passed two monks sitting in one of the carrels, talking earnestly.

By now, I was used to the strange accents of the English and had learned both to understand them and to make myself understood. I sat in a corner, intending to pray but, instead, I found myself listening to the brothers' conversation.

"Pope Innocent intends to finance his crusade by taxing the clergy: a fortieth of all income. It is unheard of. And King John, eager to win favour, has pledged to collect every penny due to Rome. There will be no exceptions. The prior is most unhappy. We are still struggling to repair the Cathedral after the fire twenty years ago."

"Don't we get enough from the guest-house?"

"Not by half. Pilgrims only pass through here on their way to Canterbury. They stay one night at most and there aren't nearly enough of them."

The other man sighed.

"We need our own saint."

"True enough. But shrines cannot be made to order. Nor saints found."

There was a thoughtful silence.

Ashamed of eavesdropping, I roused myself and went to look for my father.

I found him pacing the refectory, fretful because of the time we had wasted. I had dallied too long. Most of the pilgrims had left.

Only two remained: Reynard and his companion, a stout fellow with small, crafty eyes.

"Where have you been?" demanded my father with a flash of his old tetchiness.

I mumbled an apology.

"We must walk swiftly if we are to catch the others. I am not happy about travelling alone on the Pilgrims' road. It follows open country over the Downs and there are long distances between the villages."

"If you will permit me? We can show you a short-cut."

Bowing respectfully, Reynard stepped forward, wringing his hands like an obsequious beggar.

"No father ..."

Tugging at his sleeve, I tried to pull him away, but he brushed me off.

"Hush, boy. This is our only choice," he muttered.

"Thank you, my friend. I am grateful for your offer. We will accompany you."

Reynard smiled, slyly, giving his companion a sideways glance. The other man grunted, his small pigs' eyes glittering behind arrow-slit lids.

***

Our route from Rochester should have run east. But the two men led us south. My misgivings grew. I was not convinced by Reynard's short-cut.

But my father was in good spirits. Reynard kept him amused with lively stories, while his companion placed himself between us, separating me from my father. I could neither speak to him nor catch his eye. I trailed along silently, berating myself for having wasted time in the cloisters.

Every so often, my father would laugh heartily, tears of mirth running down his cheeks. Reynard was a skilled storyteller and he could bewitch a listener with his tales. But, as he talked, he sidled closer to my father, eyeing the scrip hanging from his belt: the wallet that held all our money.

A few miles out of the city, the road began to twist, meandering without purpose; more of a sheep-track than a highway, a rutted lane flanked by high banks and hedges where only two men could walk abreast. Reynard and my father led the way and I, uneasy, walked behind with Reynard's companion.

It all happened so quickly. As my father threw back his head to laugh at another of Reynard's tales, the large man pushed me aside and struck him on the head.

One blow from that fist would have felled a calf. Stunned, my father sank to his knees. Leaping forward, Reynard grasped his hair and pulled his head back; then, pulling a knife from his tunic, he slashed his throat.

As my father lay senseless in the road, they stripped him of his wallet, regardless of the pool of blood growing around their feet.

Stricken with terror, I ran: leaping ditches, forcing my way through hedges and brambles until finally,

I found shelter in a small copse where I lay panting and terrified, praying that they would not follow me.

I hid there for hours, startled by the crackle of every twig, the scuffling of birds in the undergrowth, the cawing of rooks overhead, even the whisper of dead leaves stirred by the wind.

At any moment, I expected to hear the murderers' footfall, to feel sharp steel at my throat. I shivered uncontrollably, more from fear than the cold; my teeth chattering like a bag of loose nails.

Finally, having gathered my wits, I crawled from my lair. Seeking the cover of hedges and banks, I crept back to where my father's body lay, now cold and caked in blood. I stared at him from behind a hedgerow and was about to step into the road when I heard footsteps.

A woman, filthy and dressed in rags, staggered into view. Seeing the body in the road, she dropped to her knees and crawled towards my father. Cautiously, reaching out a finger, she prodded him then, grasping his arm, shook him vigorously. Perplexed at the lack of response, she whined like a dog. Then, with a tender movement, she stroked his head.

"Wake up, love. Wake up!"

His body lay motionless. Rocking back on her heels, she gave a low, keening wail. Then, crawling to the verge, she tore handfuls of wildflowers and scattered them over his wounds.

"That'll cure him."

Retrieving a few of the flowers from the corpse, she threaded them through her hair, teasing buttercups into the matted knots, weaving daisies into the tallow strings about her face.

"A cure. A cure," she sang to herself. "I cure him. He cures me."

But my father did not move.

Getting to her feet, the woman swayed a little, humming to herself, unsure of her direction. Then, she saw something that pleased her and, holding out her arms, ran forward. I could not see the object of her pleasure, but I could hear voices.

Moments later, the woman returned, accompanied by two monks in black habits; Benedictines from the priory at Rochester.

"Say, woman! Did you have any part in this?"

The man spoke harshly. I recognised him as one the brothers whose conversation I had overheard in the cloisters.

"He cured me. He cured me," pleaded the woman.

She did not understand the question but, sensing some danger to herself, became anxious. Picking the wilted flowers from her hair, she twisted them between her fingers.

"He cured me," she murmured. "I cure him. He cures me."

"It's all right, Bess. Calm yourself."

The other monk patted the woman's arm.

"I know this woman, Brother Robert. She is easily confused but there is no harm in her. She often comes to the priory for food."

"Hmm."

Brother Robert seemed unconvinced. He was older and senior in status to his companion. His lean, clever face was shaped by intellect rather than kindness and no emotion stirred in his cool eyes.

He bent to examine the body, undeterred by the bloody wounds. Parting the matted hair with his fingers, he pressed my father's scalp with his fingers, then turned the body over to inspect the gash in his throat.

"Wounds of this kind would have required a good

deal of force. One man, possibly two. Even with her wits about her, this woman would not have been able to inflict such injuries."

Rising to his feet, he regarded the corpse thoughtfully.

"I will speak on this woman's behalf to the sheriff. He will listen to me. But any others travelling this road today will fall under suspicion."

I held my breath, trying not to make a sound. Surely, as my father's companion, I would be the first to be suspected of his murder.

"Come. Let us return to the priory. I will send the ostler with a cart to collect the body. This man was a pilgrim and may be known to the brothers at the guest-house. At least, we can give him a Christian burial."

As he turned to go, I glimpsed his face. He was deep in thought. An idea was forming behind those cold, blue eyes.

The younger monk put his arm around the woman's shoulders.

"Come with us, Bess. The prior may wish to speak to you. But there is nothing to be afraid of. I will find you food and a bed for the night in the guest-house."

"Food?" enquired the woman, hopefully.

"And a bath, too, God willing," added the older monk.

***

I waited for half an hour until I was sure that it was safe to leave my hiding place, then I crept over to where my father lay. But I did not recognise him in that cold corpse. Death had divested him of everything familiar. All anger, shame and desire had left him. He was no more to me now than a carcase on a butcher's block.

I struggled to cry, but no tears came. I felt curiously calm. Even relieved. I said a prayer over him, then left. Climbing through the hedge, I set out in what I judged to be the right direction.

After travelling many miles through fields and woods, I eventually found my way back onto the old Roman road. There, shock and the lack of food caught up with me. My stomach ached with hunger and my legs felt weak. Too tired even to seek shelter, I sat down beside the road and fell asleep.

***

The heavy crunch of wheels entered my dreams. Drowsily, I opened my eyes. A cart loaded with sacks was grinding towards me. I awoke instantly. I was far from any lodging and without food or money. This was my only chance.

In desperation, I leapt into the road, forcing the carter to halt. He was a red-cheeked, choleric fellow and, at first, I thought he might turn his whip on me. So I talked fast, stumbling over the English words, assuring him that I meant no harm.

At first, he looked at me askance, wondering if I was a runaway from a great lord's manor. But I told him that I was a pilgrim who had been robbed of his possessions – a story that was all too common; and that, together with my foreign accent, persuaded him that I was telling the truth.

Besides, I represented a bargain: a ride in return for free labour; the only price for my work being a lump of stale bread, a rind of cheese and some watery ale from his own bottle.

After two days, we arrived in Canterbury. By then, we had struck up a friendship of sorts and he offered to take me with him to Dover. But I wanted to explore the City, seeking my fortune in the shadow of the Cathedral.

"Hmmph. Young lads. All the same," grumbled the carter. But he flung me a halfpenny as he drove away.

***

It had rained overnight and, despite the early hour, the narrow streets of Canterbury had already been mashed to a muddy pulp by wagons, horses and the feet of pilgrims.

I breakfasted on a lump of grey bread and some hard cheese – a gift from the carter – and washed it down with some weak ale bought from one of the stalls that lined the streets.

There were many goods to tempt pilgrims: hats, staves, leather bags, purses, cloaks, shoes, sandals, pies, bread and honey. There were souvenirs, too: small pewter ampullae, water bottles which could be filled with holy water from the shrine and carried home for the benefit of a sick friend or relative.

Before me, the stone bulwark of the Cathedral towered over the hovels clustered below: a hen with many chicks. I followed the pilgrims streaming through its portals, eager to see the shrine of Saint Thomas Becket.

Surrounded by travellers from many countries who chattered in strange tongues, I felt a thrill of excitement. It was unlike any of the other shrines that I had visited. This was not the tomb of some long-dead saint, but of a man who had died less than 30 years ago, whose contemporaries were still living. A man like us.

Although he had been a cleric, Saint Thomas was no hermit. He had not divorced himself from the world, but lived within it. His father had been a merchant and property-owner and Thomas, himself, had been Lord Chancellor of England: a man of affairs. That was something the stall-holders outside could understand. He was close to us both in time and experience. His suffering at the hands of a tyrant earned him the sympathy of at least one baker's boy.

When my time came, I knelt before the magnificent tomb inlaid with jewels and tried to pray for my father. I clenched my fists, digging my nails into my palms. Yet it was not Christ's passion that transported me, but my own; a powerful current that carried me off on its heaving back, far from grace.

Saint Thomas may have forgiven his tormentor, but I could not. Transfigured by rage, I could pray neither for my father nor myself.

I sprang to my feet and strode angrily out of the Cathedral, pushing past the lonely and unloved, despising the sick, stepping over beggars with their hands outstretched. Their misery infuriated me because it reminded me of my own. I wanted to blot it out.

Drink, women, violence: at that moment I would

have tried anything to silence the screaming in my head. To my horror, I began to understand what had made my father act as he did.

I was his son and I hated him because I was made in his image. I could see it in my face and feel it in my bones. William lived on in me. I would never escape him. Even death could not separate us.

***

Blindly, I ran through the narrow streets, without direction, not caring where I was going. Finally, breathless and exhausted, I leant against the wall of a house at the corner of a small alley. I closed my eyes and let the street invade my senses.

The sun had grown hot and I could feel the warm plaster of the wall through my shirt. Two dogs were snarling over a bone, a girl was singing and sparrows chirped in the rafters overhead. Above the rattling of cartwheels, a woman shrieked from a window to her neighbour and church bells clanged in unison from many towers.

Then, above the cabbage-rotten stench of the gutters, I recognised a familiar smell. Bread.

Drawn by its ancient magic, I followed the familiar aroma of yeast and flour. Half-way down the alleyway, I found an open-fronted shop and, feeling the blast of warm air on my skin, peered into the dark interior. The baker, his friendly face spattered with flour, was pounding dough in a deep wooden trough.

Cautiously, I stepped inside and offered my services. He clapped his hands and laughed. I was the answer to a prayer. He worked alone and the pilgrims' demand for bread exceeded his capacity. He had been looking for an assistant and was delighted to find one already skilled in the trade.

***

From that day, my luck changed. I thrived with my new master and eventually married his daughter, Alice: a sweet, plump girl with pink cheeks and flaxen hair, whose kindness won my devotion and whose laughter put dark thoughts to flight.

But for all her gentle ministrations, Alice could not soothe my nightmares. William stalked my dreams, wordlessly reproaching me for having left him on the road. Every night in my sleep, I was called back to that deserted country lane to witness my father's murder.

Struck dumb, my limbs frozen, I could neither run nor shout for help. Again and again, I would see the knife flash and the blood spurt from his throat. Then, I would wake choking on my screams, bathed in a lather of sweat.

Even the living returned to haunt me.

One day as I walked through the Buttermarket, I saw two familiar faces: Reynard and his companion, skulking by the Cathedral gate, eyeing up new victims.

Reynard recognised me and pulling his accomplice by the sleeve, dived into the crowds, running swiftly into the maze of small streets that surrounded the Cathedral. I had no wish to follow – or have my throat cut in some dark alley – so I hurried home.

After that, I was confined to the house for many days, tormented by visions of the past, unable to eat or speak. Despite my love for Alice, I could not share my secret. I would not let the shadows from my past dim her brightness.

I can only suppose that Reynard and his companion were as terrified of me as I of them. For, after that, I never saw them again, nor heard any more of their dark deeds.

But I did hear more of my father.

In the course of my trade, I spoke to many pilgrims and I began to hear tales of another miraculous tomb. At Rochester. It belonged to a pilgrim who had been murdered on his way to Becket's shrine.

Such was the man's sanctity that the mere touch

of his dead body had cured a mad woman. Others had been cured, too. He was sure to become a saint.

His name?

William of Perth.

***

Years later, I had occasion to visit Rochester: a matter of business as my bakery was thriving. But I was also drawn by curiosity.

At first, my father's death left me numb. After that, haunted by blood-soaked dreams, I felt revulsion and anger. Yet, as time passed and I became father to my own child, William's words of contrition came back to me; a faint, tantalising echo.

I remembered his confession by the fire at our home in Perth. Gradually, I began to understand how a man can be stricken and twisted by love rather than healed by it. William had been one of those men. He had tormented and beaten me. Yet, towards the end, I knew he loved me.

I clung to that knowledge, keeping it alive, letting it burn inside me like a tiny votive flame, small and constant: a pinpoint of light in the darkness.

As the rumours of William's martyrdom grew, I felt myself drawn back to him. Yet I struggled against it. For other words also lingered from the past: those of the monks who discovered William's body. *Any others travelling this road today will fall under suspicion.*

For many years, fearing that I might be accused of William's murder, I had revealed little of my former life. No-one, not even my wife or her father, knew of my connection to him.

But, by now, my appearance had changed. Age had etched lines on my face, tweaked out my hair and fattened my belly. I was no longer recognisable as the skinny boy who had accompanied my father and my command of English was now akin to that of a native. Few knew that I came from Scotland. Those who did had forgotten.

And so, on a bright spring morning, I set out for Rochester with my wife Alice and our young son, Andrew. We were merry and the sun waxed hot as we bumped along the road in our cart, past hedges foaming with blackthorn blossom.

In Scotland, this was the sign to sow barley and I remembered how, in my native tongue, blackthorn was known as *straif* or the *slae tree*. Strife and slay. It reminded me of that terrible day on a deserted road when two men had set upon my father and, in my terror, I had fled.

I had always assumed that William was the sinner

and that, in all things, I was blameless. But perhaps he had not been the only one at fault. If cowardice is a sin, there was something for which I, too, needed forgiveness.

Other questions followed, unbidden. As a boy my hatred burned hot and I wondered if there had been another reason for abandoning William that day.

Had I been prompted by pique because he had not listened to my warning? Had I wanted to teach him a lesson: to pay him back for all the misery he had inflicted? Was this the reason for my terrible dreams?

I flicked the reins sharply. The horse's loin twitched. Beside me, Alice and Andrew laughed and chattered unaware of the storm that was raging in my head. I did my best to conceal my torment from them, for I was not a man to sully the happiness of others: but dark thoughts pursued me all the way to Rochester.

***

I noticed a change as soon as we entered the City. Many little booths and stalls had sprung up at the roadside; housewives were selling ale and pies from the windows of their houses and there was such a press of people in the High Street that it took us many minutes to cover the short distance to the Priory guest-house. That, too, had changed. It was bigger, having been extended to twice its previous size, with more space for sleeping, eating and stabling horses.

I did not see either of the monks who had discovered William's body. But the Guest-Master was a talkative fellow and, without being prompted, told us how the City had benefited from William's shrine.

Pilgrims were flocking to William's tomb in increasing numbers, offering candles and prayers. There were so many visitors that the Priory guest-house overflowed, even in winter. Building projects at the Cathedral were flourishing and the town was full of masons and stone-cutters, glass-workers, roofers and carpenters.

Having rested and eaten, I was impatient to visit the shrine.

"Goodness," said Alice. "I never remember you being in such a hurry to say your prayers."

But, with her usual good nature, she fell in with my plans. Leading Andrew by the hand, we elbowed our way through streets teeming with pedlars, pilgrims, monks, nuns, gypsies, drovers, sailors, soldiers, housewives, husbands and whores.

At every turn, our noses were assaulted by the aroma of hot pies, baking bread and roasting meat as well as the stench of animal dung and rotting refuse.

Finally, we reached the north door of the Cathedral where, joining a long queue of pilgrims, we slowly filtered inside. The interior was dark and airless, filled with the heat of many candles, the murmur of prayers and the scent of incense which overlay – but failed to banish – the smell of sweat and unwashed bodies.

Alice and Andrew gazed around, their mouths open in wonder. I thought of that morning years ago, when I overheard two monks talking in the cloisters.

The man behind nudged me in the back, urging me forward. We followed the flow of pilgrims up a set of shallow steps already shiny with much use. Before us was a huge granite coffin. This, too, shone; polished to a patina by the touch of many hands, pilgrims praying for relief from their suffering; all trying to get nearer to William the martyr; my father.

At the foot of the tomb were many candles and, beyond them, a crowd of kneeling figures. I, too, touched the tomb and knelt before it.

"Forgive me," I murmured.

And suddenly, fear and anger left me, pouring

from my heart in a black torrent. At last, I could grieve for my father: a man who was weak and imperfect; a bully, a beater, a killer; a practised sinner, despicable and fallen from grace; but one who had finally found the courage to admit his wickedness and seek mercy. In a sense, he had died for his sins. But had he not also died for me? Or perhaps because of me?

I realised now that it was his love of me that had made him listen. He had sold his bakery and come on pilgrimage. To please me. To earn my forgiveness. That love had led him to his death: a violent, lonely martyrdom on a country road far from help. And in his need, I had deserted him.

At last, it lay revealed. The seed of my suffering. Guilt.

"Forgive me," I sobbed. "Forgive me, father."

Then, amid the violence of my grief, a voice:

All who repent will be forgiven.

Startled, I turned to see who had spoken. But I could see no-one.

I had spoken those words to William long ago. And now, across a chasm of time, they had returned. Was it my voice that I had heard? Or his?

It did not matter. I had been released.

Clutching Alice's hand, I got shakily to my feet and let her lead me outside. Beneath a twisted pear tree, we found a seat on a low wall. I slumped down, sack-like, clinging to the rough brick with my fingers and gasping the cool air into my lungs.

The sunlight pierced my gloom-deadened eyes and I felt as if my head would burst. Weak and shaking, I wept again while Andrew, awed by a father's grief, peered at me over Alice's shoulder.

Alice held me until my sobbing abated. The poison was gone. I was filled with quiet bliss; a memory that, until now, had been forgotten, buried beneath images of brutality. It was something that I had experienced on my earlier trip to Rochester with William when I had heard the monks sing at Prime. Peace. A promise of heaven.

As the pear tree scattered its blossom on our heads, I examined the tiny violets peeping from crevices in the wall and, with my finger, followed the silvery passage of snails that criss-crossed its surface.

"Better now?" asked Alice, drying my cheek with her sleeve.

But she had already seen the change in me. She placed her hand on my chest, sensing that the darkness had left my heart.

"William must have been a very good man," she said, staring deep into my eyes. "He's cured you."

I roared with laughter.

"What's so funny?" she asked.

I kissed her, still laughing, convulsed with joyful irony.

For, in some measure, we had all got what we wanted. William had the renown he craved. The monks had their saint. And I had my freedom.

A miracle indeed!

Homeward Bound

A Riddle: Who am I?

The treasure which inspired this story has strong connections with Anglo-Saxon England. For that reason, I took my inspiration for this piece from an Anglo-Saxon riddle. In telling its story, the treasure gives clues to its identity. To avoid spoiling the fun, I have reversed the order of content followed elsewhere in this book.

Homeward Bound

I am sleepy now. It's quiet in here. They still treat me with reverence and speak in hushed voices; just as they did in my old home. But there, I had more visitors. Here, I may not see anyone for weeks. Just the cleaning lady; a young girl who has music piped into her ears from a machine to drown out the noise of another machine, the Hoover.

These days, it seems that there is no place for silence; at least not the contemplative kind. That silence was filled with thought. It was companionable and could be shared with others. Today's silence is empty, a badge of neglect; deserted streets, derelict lives. No-one wants to share that. It is something to fear, to be fought with noise: radio, television, the telephone. People drown their own thoughts in a wave of sound, creating the very thing they dread: loneliness.

Hush! I can see a light under the door. Voices. I have a visitor. It's the doctor; a thin man in his fifties. His head is covered with wisps of rusty hair, the same colour as his corduroy jacket and the frames of his glasses. Apart from these muted highlights, he is devoid of colour. Like me he is invisible, filled with knowledge for which no-one has any use. But I like him. He has gentle hands. I tingle when he touches me, for he reminds me of another: the first man to caress my skin, the one who made me what I am.

For I have a story to tell. It is an interesting one, full of intrigue and adventure.

***

He tickled me with a bird's feather, that first one. He scratched me too. But it was all in the cause of beauty: at least, as far as I was concerned. I was very fussy about my appearance. I would not countenance a blemish of any kind. In those days, I had the vanity of a young girl. Every mark, tattooed onto my skin had to be perfect. So I lay very still while work was in progress.

We spent many hours together; alone, late into the night, keeping our trysts by the light of a candle. A love affair, of sorts, that lasted many years. I was his work of art, that's what he called me. He even told me once, that I was the love of his life. And him, a man forbidden to marry!

While my skin remained pure and seamless, his began to wrinkle. First, little cracks around the eyes, then the mouth. And the colour in his cheeks, once so fresh and rosy, began to fade. Our time was passing. And I grieved. But he poured his life into me. As he grew thin, I grew fat. As his energy waned, I became stronger, my body girded with leather and metal.

And then, one day, he did not return and another

took up his work. It was never the same after that. No-one had his devotion. Or his touch. My first and only love.

***

I was a beauty with pride of place in the Great House, shown off to all, including kings. I alone had the power to defy royal pretenders. The possessor of many lands, I defeated their greedy schemes. My word was law and I taught them the meaning of justice.

Criminals were brought before me for judgement and I decided the means of their trial. Water, iron or something a little more irregular: a diet of barley bread and cheese, something so subtle that even my current doctor cannot grasp it.

Yet that humble ordeal felled a mighty nobleman. Earl Godwin, father of King Harold, was accused of murder. He chose the ordeal of barley bread and cheese and scoffed at it. Yet scoffing was his downfall. He ate one mouthful and dropped down dead.

***

All men wished to possess me. I visited London on several occasions where I was measured for new clothes and my likeness recorded for posterity. I was the talk of the town, examined, admired and, although passed from hand to hand, always treated with respect. Except on one occasion.

In London, I was taken to visit a friend who was to escort me home. However, my friend was absent from his lodgings, so I was left to await his return. The landlady said she would look after me. Unscrupulous jade! No sooner were we alone, than she forced me up the stairs and began to pound on the door of another lodger.

Dr Thomas Leonard was a physician from Canterbury. The sight of me took his breath away. I shuddered as he pawed me with his greasy fingers. My beautiful skin! The doctor said that I was a rare specimen and struck a bargain with the landlady for five shillings. I was bought and sold like a slave-girl in a market. It was a dark chapter in my history.

After that, men quarrelled over me like dogs over a bone. I was taken to the Court of Chancery where lawyers in powdered wigs argued in a language that I could not understand. For days, they strutted about in a foul-smelling, airless room: presenting arguments, interrogating witnesses; crows who believed themselves peacocks displaying to an empty gallery.

This long-winded, meandering justice was new to me. It did not have the immediacy of the ordeal. No blood-curdling test for truth or lies. Rather the combatants wore each other down by talking.

On and on they went. In a way, I suppose it was a kind of ordeal. The judge certainly thought so. Constantly yawning and rubbing his eyes, he had perfected the art of napping while appearing to nod sagely. But, occasionally, his snoring betrayed him!

At last, justice triumphed and I was taken home. And then came the final insult.

On one of my last outings, they dropped me in the river! Do not ask how it happened. I cannot remember. But as I sank through the murky depths, I thought that I had breathed my last. In the filthy mire of the Thames, I felt cold water lapping around me. Barges, cutters, ferries and row-boats: the hulls of boats passed overhead while small fish began to nibble at my skin.

It took them hours to rescue me. When they finally hauled me to safety, they wondered how I had survived. But all I had to show for my ordeal was a light, crystalline powder that gave my skin a delicate glow.

Once again, I was ahead of my time. It would take them over two hundred years to perfect anything like it for other women. And they would call it make-up and talk about it as if it was something new. Honestly!

But that's all in the past.

As I said, I don't have many visitors now. I'm in a home for the elderly. Like them, I've lost my voice. Few understand what I say. Only a few enthusiastic doctors who come to examine me. They're especially interested in my tattoos. Carolingian minuscule, they call it. They say it displays unique characteristics. And they still marvel at my speech: Old English with a touch of Jutish. Rather rare, I'm told.

I spend most of my days sleeping. And I dream of going home. To the Cathedral where once I sat on the presbytery altar. Who knows? Perhaps, one day, there will be a new chapter in the life of this old book.

The Treasure: Who am I?

The subject of the riddle is a very special book: the *Textus Roffensis*. Written at Rochester, it dates from the 12th century and contains one of the most complete collections of Anglo-Saxon law. Apart from a few later additions, this unique manuscript was the work of a single scribe at the Benedictine Priory of St Andrew which was adjacent to Rochester Cathedral. It consists of 235 leaves and is written on vellum, that is, sheets of specially-prepared calf-skin.

When reading a brief history of the *Textus Roffensis*, I was struck by the book's extraordinary adventures. It was lent to various scholars and travelled up to London on a number of occasions for re-binding and copying. It became the subject of at least two custody disputes, one of which led to a legal battle in the Court of Chancery.

To add to the excitement, the book was accidentally ducked in a river (either the Thames or the Medway). Its survival on that occasion was thought to be largely due to brass clasps which bound its pages so tightly that water could not penetrate beyond the outer margins.

Sadly, this wonderful old book now resides, not at its place of origin, but in the Medway Archive at Strood. This is, no doubt, a safe environment; but, from the book's point of view, it is probably somewhat dull compared to its colourful history.

When writing this story, it seemed appropriate to compare the *Textus Roffensis* to an old person dreaming of the past and a much-loved, former home: in this case, Rochester Cathedral.

Barley Bread and Cheese

The Treasure: The Textus Roffensis

The *Textus Roffensis* not only records a number of charters relating to Cathedral lands (very useful for proving ownership in cases of dispute) but, more importantly, it is thought to provide one of the most complete records of Anglo-Saxon law. These include the Laws of King Aethelbert dating from 604 AD as well as the laws of other Kentish kings from the 7th and 8th centuries.

Among the old laws recorded by the *Textus Roffensis* are those grouped together under the title Iudicia Dei or Judgements of God. These refer to the ordeals by which the guilt or innocence of those accused of crime was put to the test. Most commonly these ordeals consisted of holding red-hot iron, immersing one's hand in boiling water or of the individual being totally immersed in water.

However, there is one ordeal that has perplexed historians for centuries. It is that of barley bread and cheese: an ordeal known as *corsned* in Old English. How this ordeal was supposed to have worked and who was subjected to it is still a matter of conjecture. While some commentators maintain that it was reserved for members of the clergy, there is also a famous example of it being applied to a layman.

Godwin, earl of Kent, the father of King Harold, was accused of murdering his own brother. He elected to take the ordeal of barley bread and cheese to prove his innocence. Before submitting himself to the ordeal, he cried: "May this bread choke me if I am guilty!" It did and Godwin died.

The mystery that surrounds this ordeal provided the theme for my story. Here, a young historian finds a novel application for an ancient test of truth.

Barley Bread and Cheese

At last, a table!

We had waited twenty minutes, squeezed onto a stairwell that resembled Jacob's Ladder. Shuffling back and forth, we had tucked in our elbows and sucked in our breath, dodging the constant traffic of waitresses, customers, children, push-chairs and carry-cots that flowed past in both directions.

I had been squashed against a woman in a duffle-coat that reeked of wet Alsatian. She had finally given up: rotating slowly, disengaging from the queue, then pushing past me down the stairs; her soft, puff-pastry face crimped with discontent.

"Can't wait all day," she muttered. "Got a bus to catch."

We moved to the front of the queue, stepping off the stairwell into the tea-shop where customers clustered around gingham-draped tables, gorging on tea, cakes and gossip.

By the window, a couple rose from their table: she, chattering constantly, mustering the carrier bags herded around her feet; he, listening intently, hands in pockets, slightly stooped. Swapping items from one bag to another, she tested them for weight, balancing them in either hand like a set of human scales. Yet, for all her fussing, she never took her eyes from his face. He returned her gaze, calm and constant.

Both middle-aged, past their prime, slightly tousled, probably in need of a good wash. Not dirty exactly, but the sort who followed a one-bath-a-week routine with flannel washes on the other six days. A war-time ethic, probably inherited from their parents.

The woman was plump with a round face; no make-up; a crumpled coat and a scraggle of hair whose only purpose was to cover her head. The man, lean and rangy, wore black jeans and a mock leather jacket. His greying quiff hinted at Elvis, his sunken cheeks at decay: either teeth or something more deep-rooted.

They made an unlikely pair. But they loved each other. That was clear. It amused me in my youthful arrogance. How could two such unlovely people share such deep affection? I felt a strange pang of jealousy, a fleeting emptiness like a dark hole in the pit of my stomach.

As they jostled past, the woman beamed at me, her fat cheeks like two round, pink cakes. The man winked, not flirtatious but as if he read my thoughts.

"You'll find out," he seemed to say. "One day you'll understand."

He coughed as he went past; a deep, rattling hack tainted with tobacco.

"Look, a table by the window!" Ailish declared.

She darted across the room, expertly weaving her way around chairs and tables, hopping over bags and evading the sharp looks of the waitress who expected her customers to behave in an orderly manner.

I followed, smiling sheepishly at the waitress who pretended to ignore me.

The table was still littered with coffee cups rimed with stale froth, dirty plates and trails of sugar that had spilled from discarded paper sachets.

The waitress stumped towards us bearing a tray. With an obtrusive clatter, she piled up the dirty crockery, sweeping the crumbs off the table with her hand, careless of whether or not they landed in our laps.

"I'll be back in a minute to take your order," she snapped.

"Hope she doesn't spit in the tea," hissed Ailish.

We sniggered like guilty schoolgirls.

There was something timeless about that small,

first-floor room with its creaking floorboards – something that defied the ceaseless advance of New World coffee-shops with their Moccachino language: grande, latte, americano. This was a traditional tea-shop and it spoke plain English.

The cakes were displayed under glass domes ranged along the shelves, not in chiller cabinets. They had simple titles: coffee-and-walnut, lemon drizzle, Victoria sponge. There were no transatlantic imposters here: no death-by-chocolate, cupcakes or brownies. Just Old World cake of doorstep proportions.

These royal confections were supported by a yeomanry of lesser treats, plain but substantial: Eccles cakes, shortbread, scones and cheese on toast. You could even get sardines. Or a boiled egg with soldiers.

"What are you having?" I asked, although it was a foregone conclusion.

"Cream cakes," came the reply.

Ailish maintained her flawless skin, silky blonde hair and delicate figure on a diet of sugar, starch and dairy. More specifically, cream cakes. She demanded them wherever she went. Even on academic conferences in far-flung parts of the world, she would order – and get – cream cakes for breakfast.

I ordered fruit scones with butter, no jam. My tastes have always been simple.

The waitress took our order, scratching it onto a small note-pad which, like her pencil stub, was kept in the pocket of her white pinafore. Her uniform consisted of a black dress and frilly head-band, reminiscent of a Lyons Nippy.

"Good, now that's done, I can read through my notes."

Ailish pulled a sheaf of papers from the battered old music case that she took everywhere. Dismissive of technology, she insisted on carrying notebooks, pens, photocopies and pencil-sharpeners on every study trip.

One of the photocopied sheets dropped onto the table: the illustration of a saint accompanied by a dragon. I recognised it instantly. It was a page from the *Textus Roffensis*; the precious 12th century manuscript written by a monk in the priory of Rochester Cathedral.

The *Textus* was the subject of my PhD thesis. Every detail was inscribed on my memory: the purposeful stroke of the scribe's pen; the unique collection of Anglo-Saxon laws; the copy of Henry I's Coronation Charter in which he promised to govern justly in an attempt to win his subjects' support.

I had never liked Henry. He had sneaked onto the throne while his elder brother Robert had been away on Crusade. But this was only to be expected of a son of William the Conqueror. None of our Norman kings suffered from a queasy conscience.

For some reason, the thought of Henry made me uneasy. To my mind, the betrayal of a family member or friend ranked as one of the most heinous crimes. The idea that you could not trust anyone – even those closest to you – was deeply troubling.

But Henry was the least of my problems. I had reached a point in my research which appeared to be a dead end. The *Textus Roffensis* had set me an academic teaser. Among its miscellany of texts was a section called the Iudicia Dei or Judgements of God. These consisted of a list of 'ordeals'; crude trials of guilt in criminal cases.

They included being bound and thrown into a river, plunging your hand into boiling water or being forced to carry a quantity of red-hot iron. Your reaction to the challenge was the measure of your guilt or innocence.

By inflicting extreme pain, the ordeals were intended to test both truthfulness and good character. Despite their brutality, they had an innate logic. But there was one that perplexed me.

"Ailish, have you got any thoughts on the barley bread and cheese ordeal?"

Bemused, she looked up, her brow wrinkled in a charming frown.

"The what?"

"You know. The ordeal where the defendant is made to eat barley bread and cheese. I don't understand it. It's not like any of the others. In fact, I can't see how it could be an ordeal at all."

"Hmmm," she looked thoughtful. "If you refused to eat it, you were found guilty."

"Yes, but it sounds more like a reward for a starving peasant. Who would ever refuse to eat barley bread and cheese? It seems like a very easy test. Impossible to fail."

"Well, I suppose if the bread was really stale and the cheese was rotten and you were expected to eat a large quantity of it ... "

She smiled impishly as a new idea formed.

"Or perhaps the defendant was known to have a wheat and dairy intolerance!"

"Ailish, really!"

We both giggled. She poured herself another cup of tea.

"Actually, it might not have been so silly. Do you remember that Christmas party at my flat when you, Sam and I had a bet to see if anyone could eat a whole packet of Cornish wafers, without butter or a glass of water?"

I vaguely recalled the event.

"We couldn't manage it though, could we?" I mused.

"No, you're wrong," Ailish contradicted. "I challenged Sam to eat them all. And he did. Don't you remember?"

Now I did.

Ailish bent over her music case and began rummaging about inside, her hair falling forward over her face.

"Anyway," she mumbled, "I'm sure there was some trick of making barley bread and cheese into a real ordeal. We just don't have the information."

I pushed back the damp, yellow curtain. The window was bedewed with condensation; the moist working of many mouths in an enclosed space.

I rubbed a clear patch with my hand and peered down at the small narrow street.

From the pavement, stone steps led to an overcast garden where pansies shivered around a war memorial. Beyond that, the grey mass of the Cathedral burst from the ground; an eruption of stone, defying gravity, frozen in flight.

Strange how this ancient building had brought us together: my fiancé Sam, Ailish and me. Although we were almost contemporaries, Ailish was our tutor. A leading authority on medieval manuscripts, she was already a professor at a local university.

One of the growing clan of media academics, she had already been courted by a television producer who had tried to woo her away from academe – and into his bed – with the inducement of her own series.

However, Ailish had broken the news to him, politely but firmly, that her career path would not be determined by her choice of bedfellows.

"I said I'd sleep with him on one condition. I'd set him a challenge, a test of endurance. At his expense, we would go to a smart hotel and order a gargantuan cream tea. With me as his witness, he would be subjected to the Ordeal of Twelve Cream Cakes. And he would have to eat the lot. Sadly for him, he fell at the second éclair."

She had forced him to sit and watch, miserable and deflated, as she had eaten all the remaining cakes, then licked the cream from her fingers. Ailish always laughed when she recounted this story. She told it again today. But with an addendum.

"There has only ever been one man who could complete that test."

"And did he get his reward?"

"Oh yes."

Balancing a white sugar lump on her tea-spoon, she dunked it briefly in the tea and watched as the liquid seeped upwards, turning the sugar brown.

"Who was it?"

The spoon dropped into the cup, spattering the table-cloth with tea.

"No-one you know."

Preoccupied, she stirred her tea, staring at the tiny whirlpool in her cup.

I had another twinge of uneasiness. Why? Everything was fine. My work was going well – apart from the enigma of the barley bread and cheese. Sam and I were living together, due to be married next year. I had already booked venues for the service and reception. And I had chosen the dress.

Yet, recently, Sam had seemed distracted, distant. I had asked him if anything was wrong but he had avoided my questions, joking, diverting the conversation or even, on the last occasion, getting angry and storming off to the pub.

Staring into the street below, I attempted to visualise our life as a married couple. Yet the images I tried to conjure resolved into a grey, foggy veil; like the mist on the window.

Ailish's voice broke my train of thought.

"How's your work on that manuscript from Bec coming along?"

"How did you know about that?"

She shrugged, laughing.

"You told me yourself. Or had you forgotten?"

I dropped my hand into my lap to hide the fact that it was trembling. I knew that I had not told Ailish of this new piece of work. It was only an idea. And the only person I had told was Sam.

I tried to read her face, but she was staring down

into her plate, pressing stray crumbs onto the back of her fork.

"Ailish?"

"Better go," she said, dropping a £10 note onto the table. "Have this one on me. Sorry I can't stop but my train leaves in 15 minutes. See you back at college."

***

I sat on the top deck of the bus, lost in thought as it lurched around corners, jolting to a halt at traffic-lights and bus stops. It was as damp and steamy as the tea-shop, only colder. I watched a giggling teenager sigh onto the window, then trace a heart on the misted glass. She nudged her companion then wrote an arrow with a set of initials at either end.

The other girl giggled, reddened and hung her head so that her long black hair fell over her face, her shoulders trembling. With laughter? Or fear? Her tormentor was relentless. Holding up her phone to the window, she took a picture of the heart before it disappeared.

"I'm going to post this on Facebook," she teased.

"No, no," pleaded the other girl, trying to snatch away the phone.

"What's it worth?" sneered her companion.

"Please don't."

All trace of laughter had left the victim's face. She was in the other girl's power. It was a test of friendship. I waited to see what would happen.

The girl with the phone hesitated; her finger over the button, ready to send the message. There was an ominous tension, each trying to guess the other's thoughts as they anticipated the outcome. A foolish prank soon forgotten? Or a friendship destroyed?

The girl switched off her phone and put it back in her pocket. Rubbing out the heart with the sleeve of her blazer, she put her other arm around her friend.

"Don't worry, I'd never do it," she whispered.

They drew close, heads together, murmuring companionably about the secret that they shared.

As I stared at the window where the heart had been reduced to a messy smear, fragments of thought slowly coalesced. I had an idea.

***

At home, in the tiny one-bedroom flat that I shared with Sam, I set about preparing a special evening meal. I tidied up the living-room, lighting it with a selection of tea-lights and candles placed on the shelves and mantel-piece.

Robbed of bare, electric light, the room was transformed: no longer a tatty bedsit with chipped paintwork, orange and brown wallpaper and a stained carpet, but a work of faerie, a shimmering cavern.

I cleared the table, laying it carefully, polishing the glasses and cutlery to a reflective sheen. Then, I went into the kitchen where I laid out two juicy steaks on a plate. I chopped onions and fried them slowly so that, as they caramelised, they filled the flat with a mouth-watering aroma.

I could hear Sam's footsteps on the stairs, his key turning in the lock. Then, the door flew open and, accompanied by a blast of cool air, Sam appeared, his nose and cheeks nipped by the cold. He shrugged off his rucksack, flung his coat onto a chair and hurried over to the kitchen counter, eyeing the steaks.

"Mmm. My favourite. What's the occasion?"

"Oh nothing. Just go and sit down. It'll be ready soon."

I could hear him humming to himself as he walked around the bedroom: a different sound from the low mumble of his voice when he shut himself in there to make phone calls. *For work*, he always said.

I placed the steaks in the pan, listening to them sizzle gently as I delved under the sink for a domed plate cover, the sort used in restaurants. We had inherited it with the flat and I had stopped Sam from throwing it out, thinking it might come in useful.

Sam was now seated at the table.

"Any wine?" he shouted.

"In a minute. Just be patient."

The flat was filled with the delicious smell of onion and meat juices. I prepared Sam's plate, covering it with the metal dome, then bore it triumphantly into the dining-room where I placed it before him. I paused for a second, watching his eyes greedy with expectation.

"Ta da!" I swept the cover from the plate.

Sam's face fell. He looked bemused.

"What's this?" he laughed, pointing at the pile of Cornish wafers on his plate.

"A little test to show how much you love me."

"What?"

"Don't you remember? That night with Ailish. She dared you to eat a whole packet of Cornish wafers. And you did. Every last crumb."

"But that was ages ago. I was drunk."

He looked uncomfortable, started to fidget in his seat.

"Go on. Do it. If you could do it for her, you can do it for me."

"This is ridiculous!"

He pushed his chair back, ready to leave.

"No," I shouted. "You stay there. Eat them. All of them. For me."

He stared sulkily at the plate and mumbled:

"I'd rather have twelve cream cakes."

The Cinnamon Peeler's Daughter

The Treasure: Rochester Cathedral and Dickens

The Cinnamon Peeler's Daughter was written some months before the other stories in this collection. I owe the inspiration for it not just to one, but to two treasures. Together they forged a connection between my first novel *The Devil Dancers* and what was to become my second book.

I followed an extraordinary trail that led me from Ceylon – the setting of *The Devil Dancers* – to Rochester Cathedral, the central treasure of the *Barley Bread and Cheese* collection. It was another treasure that provided that vital link: Charles Dickens.

In the literary guise of Cloisterham, Rochester and its Cathedral provided the main setting for Dickens's final, unfinished novel *The Mystery of Edwin Drood*. In that book, Dickens also alludes to Ceylon: a reference that intrigued me and set me on a path that ultimately led to this collection of short stories. (See Appendix: The Ceylon Connection).

Like others who have been captivated by *The Mystery of Edwin Drood*, I found myself speculating on its outcome. It seemed to me that, even in death, Dickens had created something quite unique: a thriller without an ending which invites the reader to turn detective.

In The Cinnamon Peeler's Daughter, I explore Dickens's references to Ceylon and offer my own solution to the enduring conundrum posed by Edwin Drood.

The Cinnamon Peeler's Daughter

It is mid-summer, yet the sky begrudges its light; its dull and colourless surface unrelieved by the sun's rays or the movement of clouds. But, beneath this lifeless expanse, the world bustles. A ship glides into port, churning the leaden water with its prow, its deck-hands scurrying about like monkeys, some with ropes, some with boat-hooks, yelling, scrabbling, easing the vessel into its berth. Soon she is at rest, rolling gently with the wash from other boats, rising slowly in the water as her holds are relieved of their barrels and crates.

Now, rocked by the gentle lapping of waves, she murmurs to the vessels alongside, using that curious clinking, clanking, tinkling speech in which boats exchange stories of high winds and high seas, boasting of their exploits and how they brought their cargo safely home despite the shortcomings of their human masters.

The ship dreams of the sharp smack of salt water and the hot sun on her deck as sailors swarm about her, their cold, damp feet pattering down ladders into her hold, their quick, gnarled fingers tending her wounds. She slumbers while they swab her decks, mend her timbers and sew patches into her sails.

In a few hours, the ship's keel will sink low in the cold, grey water, weighed down by a new cargo

– and new passengers; one of whom is sitting in the parlour of one of the many inns and rest-houses ranged along the harbour, whose aim it is to provide sustenance, if not comfort, to the tide of voyagers that washes through the port.

Wrapped in a shawl, this traveller has sought privacy in a dark corner of the public-room where the door flies constantly open and shut, in response to the ebb and flow of customers. Seated at a table, she strives to write in the seam of light grudged by a small, grimy window. Before her is a plate of food, untouched and nearly cold, a slab of grey meat and a few, colourless vegetables congealed in gravy.

Heedless of the mayhem that surrounds her, the tramp of feet, the banging of the door, the inn-keeper shouting to his servant, she writes with desperate speed, her hand flying across the page, pausing occasionally at a word, then striking it out with a single deft stroke. Several sheets of paper, covered in her close, neat handwriting are arranged in a ragged pile. Her wrist is aching, but she cannot stop. The letter must be posted tonight.

Furiously she writes, on and on, until another three sheets have been filled. Then, signing her name with a flourish, she sits back and sighs, staring out of the small grimy window whose single, warped pane looks out onto a narrow alley where tradesmen, sailors, travellers, pick-pockets and charlatans mingle together, all going about their business.

As she turns her head, the dim light reveals a face of unusual darkness and exotic beauty. Some of the inmates of that dark cavern are tempted to stare, but one glance from those fierce dark eyes repels them. There is something ferocious about this delicate creature; something of the huntress.

The ink on the last page has dried. She gathers up the sheets of paper, taps them into a neat pile, then examines the letter that she has been at such pains to write, her lips moving as she reads, as if she were reciting a prayer.

The Star and Anchor Inn, Southampton
21st May, 18..
From: Miss Helena Landless
To: The Reverend Septimus Crisparkle, Minor Canon of Cloisterham Cathedral

My dear Septimus,

I am writing to you from Southampton. Tomorrow, I shall embark on a packet-boat destined for Ceylon, the country of my birth. In the hours remaining before departure, I intend to set down the reason for my return – something which I have not yet fully explained to you and which, I know, has been the cause of much sorrow. Yet it is necessary if our lives are to follow the true and honest course which we both desire.

A few days ago, you offered me all that a woman could wish: marriage, respectability beyond my station and, above all, the lifelong companionship of one whom I consider to be not only a saint, but also my brother's saviour. Yet, instead of the ready acceptance which you had every right to expect, you received a mystifying response: hesitation and a plea for more time in which to consider. By my apparent coolness, I fear that I have not only wounded you, but convinced you of my indifference.

Forgive me, dear sir, for my seeming reluctance and believe me when I say that my heart was both warm and willing – and always will be. But before I can give you a final answer, there is a matter that must first be resolved: that of my birth. For, as you know, Landless was the name of my stepfather – a cruel and brutal man. Although I know something of my real father's history, I still do not know his name. For this reason, I am not only Landless, but Nameless also. It is a matter which I know to be of great concern to your mother – and rightly so.

By marrying you in this anonymous state, I risk causing division within your family as well as embarrassment within the wider world. This I am not prepared to do. My diffidence regarding your proposal was not a sign of disinterest but of my deep affection and respect for you.

We have recently endured many trials with

regard to the matter of Mr Drood's unfortunate disappearance. I must ask your forbearance to wait a little longer while I seek to solve another mystery – that of my father's identity.

You know little of my life prior to my arrival in Cloisterham; except for what my brother, Neville, confided in you. From him you learned that our mother had died when we were young, entrusting us to a brutal stepfather whose pleasure it was to beat me while Neville looked on, helpless. You also know that we came from Ceylon. It is my intention, in this letter, to tell you as much as I know myself, in order to explain my reason for returning there.

So that you may better understand my motives, you must learn something of my mother's history; painful as it is, for me to impart.

***

My grandfather was a salagama or cinnamon-peeler. He lived in a small village, near to the southern coast of the Island, with his wife and children. The bricks of their home were built of mud and cow-dung; the floor was made of compacted soil and the roof, thatched with palm leaves.

In the dry season, the children would play outside, running and tumbling over the sun-baked earth while their mother cooked over a clay pot filled with embers. During monsoon, they sat inside, peering out at the rivers of mud that flowed up to the door and the great water-spouts that gushed from the roof, pouring down the ribs of the palm-fronds.

My country is one of extremes: tenderness and ferocity, fate and uncertainty, strength and weakness. It has but two seasons – wet and dry – and trees which, recognising no season, flower and fruit at the same time.

Ceylon's wealth has been both its strength and its frailty; a source of great riches and a lure to invaders. As kings fell to the foreign powers, so those of more humble origins attained an importance beyond their rank. So it was with my grandfather.

It was the foreign colonists, first the Portuguese and then the Dutch, who altered the course of generations and changed the fate of my grandfather and his forebears. To be born into a salagama family was not only to inherit a trade, but also a caste – a lowly one. Yet the traders' weakness became our family's strength.

The spice you call cinnamon, is called kurundu in my own tongue, Sinhalese. It is the inner bark of a tree, released from young branches by deft hammering; its fragrance is so strong that ships' captains claim to smell it many miles out to sea.

Perhaps it was this scent that haunted the dreams of traders, drawing them from the safety of their

European homes, inspiring a reckless pursuit over land and ocean until, landing on our shores they built forts to protect the spice and fought bloody battles for its possession.

For centuries, cinnamon was Ceylon's most precious commodity. Who would have thought that the fragrant bark of a tree would be more highly-prized than all the rubies, emeralds and sapphires extracted from our mines? Yet a crate of dried, brown cinnamon quills was worth more than its weight in gold.

The fortunes of the Dutch East India Company depended upon its monopoly of the cinnamon trade and, for this reason, our Dutch rulers protected both the spice and its producers. Thus, despite his low caste, my grandfather – like all salagamas – enjoyed a special status.

But this all changed under the next wave of invaders. The British succeeded the Dutch and the principle of 'laissez faire' replaced the monopoly that had favoured cinnamon-peelers, assuring them of privileges and a comfortable life. New crops, such as coffee, began to appear and plantation farming with its vast acreages and requirement for cheap, unskilled labour superseded traditional methods of production.

When cinnamon was king, even those who were not cinnamon-peelers sought to be classed as salagamas. But now, it was the salagamas who sought a new identity, doing everything they could to release their children from the clutches of the Cinnamon Department.

As Ceylon changed hands, other changes also took place. My grandfather – a reluctant convert to the Dutch Reformed Church – reverted to Buddhism, the faith of his ancestors. However, as he neared the end of his life, a missionary convinced him of the error of his ways and he converted once more to the Christian faith; although, this time, it was a British rather than a Dutch strain of Protestantism.

My grandfather died leaving a wife and five children. Unable to sustain them all, my grandmother sent the eldest out to work as servants. My mother was taken in by the same missionary who had converted her father.

Mr Sutherland and his wife were Scottish; a childless couple whose moral principles were as unyielding as the granite of their native land. Yet this severity was tempered by a love of little children; prompted, no doubt, by their own lack of them.

Although she began as a servant, my mother soon occupied the Sutherland home as its daughter, recommending herself to the couple's affections, not only by her sweet nature, but also by her readiness to learn. An able pupil, she was quick at both letters and needlework; her mind as nimble as her fingers.

As her adoptive father's sight failed, my mother would sit beside him on the verandah, describing the birds in the garden: the hoopoes, parrots and pigeons; the humming-birds sipping nectar from fragrant, trumpet-shaped flowers.

Together they would watch the rapid sunset then, taking him by the arm, she would lead him indoors to his favourite chair. After making him comfortable, she would take her place at the table where, sharing the lamplight with Mrs Sutherland, she would read aloud from the Bible; her companion nodding her approval as she sewed.

As the reverend gentleman was no longer able to write, my mother became his amanuensis, committing the sermons that he dictated to paper and, when occasion and style required, tactfully editing them.

Acting as his guide, she accompanied him to church, handing him the Bible or prayer-book from which he pretended to read, although he had long since committed their contents to memory. It was an innocent deception in which she readily participated for, as he told her, how could a blind preacher lead the heathen into light?

Among his many duties, Mr Sutherland was a

157

regular preacher at the garrison church in Kandy. Situated next to the Temple of the Tooth, the solid square tower and grey stone of the Anglican church was a stark contrast to the curving lines and golden finials of its neighbour.

No doubt the supplicants at each place of worship indulged in silent disapproval of the other, approaching their respective gods in a state of silent censure. Yet who can say if proximity to such gaudy and tantalising exoticism did not awaken something of the pagan in my mother. For it was here that she met my father, a young officer in the Royal Engineers.

Their attachment began innocently. After service, it was Mr Sutherland's practice to engage his parishioners in lengthy conversation at the church door. Tiring of the endless litany of births, marriages and deaths, my mother would wander off into the churchyard to inspect the crop of headstones whose numbers grew steadily every week. Even in death, it seems, the English must stake a claim to land, if only to a plot the length and breadth of a man's body.

She was deep in thought, contemplating the narrative on a young Captain's grave, when a voice startled her.

"Extraordinary fellow!"

It was an exclamation wrapped around an interrogative. A statement that demanded an answer.

"Yes, indeed," she murmured, her eyes still fixed upon the stone.

"I knew him, you know."

With her hand shielding her eyes from the sun, my mother turned to her companion and was confronted by a young man of middle height and upright bearing, resplendent in a red tunic with a lieutenant's insignia. The bright tropical sun glanced off his brass buttons, setting them a-twinkle so that they resembled small mirrors – the sort used by hunters to lure small birds from the safety of their perch.

With his yellow whiskers and tawny hair, there was something lion-like about this young soldier. My mother was both attracted and disturbed by him: re-assured by his strength, but also frightened by it. He seemed invincible.

With the ease of one practised in the art of pleasant conversation, he sought to engage her interest, pointing at the grave-stone.

"He died because of a wager."

"A wager?"

"Yes. His brother officers challenged him to walk all the way down to Kandy from Trincomalee – nearly a hundred miles. It was a joke – ill-conceived, but a joke nonetheless. No-one expected him to take it seriously.

"But Captain James McGlashan was not one to accept defeat. Although only twenty-seven, he was already a veteran of Waterloo and the Peninsular War with a fierce reputation for bravery. He would have died rather than accept the taint of cowardice. Even for something as trifling as a bet."

"What happened?" asked my mother, intrigued.

"Although it was the rainy season, when snakes emerge from their hiding places to inhabit the tracks and highways, he set out alone, reckless of danger, determined to complete the march. Drenched by the monsoon rain, he slept in the open with only the trees for cover and his wet clothes clinging to his skin.

"Yet, despite hardship and the ceaseless torrent falling from the skies, he continued, ploughing along roads that had turned into rivers, a prey to mosquitoes and leeches. When he arrived in Kandy he was raving and out of his wits. For days, he burned with fever until, in a moment of clarity, he asked for a priest. After receiving the last rites, he fell into a deep sleep and died."

"So sad!" exclaimed my mother.

"Yes, but he won the wager!"

Looking into the soldier's eyes, she saw that he was laughing and allowed herself a smile.

"That's better. Tell me, what is the attraction of a graveyard for such a beautiful young woman?"

Her skin darkened as the blood ran to her cheeks.

"I am the clergyman's daughter," she stammered. Then, seeing the ironic twist of his mouth, added: "His adopted daughter."

"Delighted to make your acquaintance, Miss Sutherland," said the Lieutenant with a low bow. "Allow me to escort you back to the church."

Shyly taking his arm, my mother allowed herself to be led across the coarse-bladed grass, shuddering as she passed the gravestones of five little siblings, all laid out in a row like five stone bobbins. As they approached the church, she could see her father in the porch, searching for her with faded eyes.

"I will take my leave here, Miss," said the soldier. Then leaning towards her, he whispered: "But I hope to see you again. Soon."

Clicking his heels, he winked as he saluted her. And she was lost.

The grave of Captain McGlashan became their meeting place. While Mr Sutherland conversed with his parishioners, the Lieutenant courted his daughter with small gifts: a nosegay of jasmine to pin in her black hair; love-notes written on small scraps of paper that could be concealed within a prayer-book.

She kept them all: the dried-up flowers, long since turned to dust, and the billets-doux, stored in a cigar box, which I inherited. I read them still, small scraps of yellow paper, mottled with age; brief messages – "Be Mine Forever", "Marry me!" There is also the drawing of a heart, pierced by an arrow, bearing two names; Amelia and another which, crossed through with thick pen-strokes, has been obscured.

Under the blind gaze of Mr Sutherland, somewhere between the Te Deum and the Lord's Prayer, the handsome Lieutenant persuaded my mother to run away with him. One day, after service, she slipped out of a side-door and into his arms, abandoning her former life and all who had shown her kindness.

From that day, her reputation was destroyed, her disgrace complete. I have no explanation for her actions. Indeed, she never offered one. I can only assume that the tigerish prompting of her blood overcame all ties of duty and loyalty to her protectors.

The Sutherlands were left grieving and, in the Reverend's case, obdurate. My mother was barred from their home forever, although, I believe that Mrs Sutherland secretly contrived a means of communication once she had discovered my mother's whereabouts.

But by then it was too late. My mother, having assumed matrimonial status, without the sanction of the church, had given birth to twins: my brother, Neville, and myself.

Despite many fine promises, my father never legitimised their union – or his children. My mother was an outcast, one of the growing legion of 'native wives', bound by affection – but not by law – to English men. In polite society, they were referred to as concubines; in less genteel circles, whores and prostitutes.

Seduced by empty promises, these women were simply another conquest, a further plundering of an island whose riches had been pillaged by successive waves of invaders. Gems, cinnamon, arrack and tobacco: extracted, refined, bottled and crated, then sent back home to Europe. All except the women. These, they left behind.

When Neville and I were still babies, my father's

regiment left for India. Assuring my mother that they would soon be reunited, my father arranged a temporary position for her as lady's maid to Mrs Diggory, the wife of a magistrate. But, although he promised to send my mother money so that she could follow him, neither letters nor money followed.

After waving him goodbye at the docks, she never saw nor heard from him again. Eventually, she prevailed upon the magistrate's wife – a gentle soul – to make enquiries on her behalf.

One day, Mrs Diggory came to the room in which my mother was sewing and sitting beside her, took her hand.

"My dear, he is dead."

Barely able to restrain her tears, the kindly woman told my mother what she had discovered. My father had died in the Western Ghats working on the construction of a railway.

He lies there still, buried on a mountain slope in an untended, overgrown grave alongside others who succumbed to fever or who, like him, fell to their deaths from precarious footholds.

***

Yet this was the beginning, rather than the end,

of my mother's tribulations. She owed her position to my father's friendship with Mr Diggory; a man who, despite his position of authority, was more liberal and compassionate than many of his compatriots. Fearlessly independent in his views, the magistrate was a man of high moral standing, both incorruptible and courageous. But these admirable qualities were to be his undoing.

The magistrate was responsible for the coastal district just south of the sprawling metropolis of Colombo. The main town, Negombo, consisted of little more than a road running parallel to the beach where the harsh brilliancy of the sea rivalled that of the sun and the fronds of coconut trees rattled like bones in the breeze. Yet the warm saltiness of Negombo's air offered a refuge from the stagnant vapours of the city and the pink and white villas of wealthy Britons sprang up amid the palm trees.

Few gave any thought to the other Negombo: the lawless strand whose fleet of small wooden vessels served fishermen by day and smugglers by night. Its nameless alleys, straggling down to the beach, formed a highway for illicit trade and the hovels that lined them, a refuge for thieves and murderers.

There was one, in particular: Don Pedro, the master of Negombo's criminal brotherhood. A man of some learning – and even greater cunning – he was fluent in the native languages of Tamil and Sinhala as well as English. His origin was a mystery, although his name indicates some Portuguese ancestry. In our country, names often survive as the only legacy of a forgotten race: Pereira, Fernando, Cruz.

It was rumoured that Don Pedro remained loyal to the religion of his European forefathers, making generous donations on saints' days and slipping into the local church at dusk to make his confession. Yet such observance marked the full extent of his godliness. In all other things, he led the life of a degenerate brigand.

As soon as Mr Diggory moved into the magistrate's residence, he was besieged by local people requesting favours. Every morning, they would form a long queue at the gate, hoping for a glimpse of the magistrate as he left for court in his carriage and waiting until his return when, one by one, they were allowed through the gate by his servants to present their demands.

In the first weeks of his residency, Mr Diggory had been mystified by the daily visits of a particular supplicant: an angular, hawk-nosed fellow of sallow complexion and magisterial bearing, well-dressed although his costume was a curious mix of oriental and European. Evidently a man of some substance, his presence inspired the other petitioners with awe for, however long they had been waiting, they always accorded him first place in the queue.

Each day, after bowing deeply to the magistrate,

this man would present him with a gift then leave without making any request. Soon, a tide of offerings threatened to overwhelm the house: bales of cloth, copper pans and sacks of rice flowed over from the outhouse into the scullery and two small goats gambolled about the yard, trying to eat the washing from the line while hens cackled in cages piled against a wall.

Puzzled by this behaviour and unable to engage the man in conversation, the magistrate asked one of his servants to explain.

"Ah," said the man, looking slyly at his master. "That is Don Pedro, sir. A very powerful man. He wishes to enter an agreement."

"What sort of agreement?"

"He is a man of business. He wishes you to be his partner."

"In return for what?"

"Your silence, sir," the servant replied, simply.

"And what is Don Pedro's business?" demanded the magistrate, his cheeks flushing angrily.

The servant shrugged as if no explanation were necessary.

"What sort of business?" demanded Mr Diggory.

"Buying, selling, contraband, all types of thievery."

The man gave Mr Diggory a sideways grin and winked, slyly.

"How dare you! How dare you suppose ..."

Furious, Mr Diggory raised his fist as if to strike the man. Quaking, the servant wrapped his arms about his head to shield himself from the blows. Confronted with this quivering, pathetic creature, the magistrate was moved to pity.

"The fault is mine," he murmured, lowering his arm. "I have been a fool."

The servant peeped out between his hands, curious to see what would happen next.

"I suppose," ventured the magistrate, "that Don Pedro is your master?"

"Yes, sir. You and Don Pedro are both my masters," affirmed the servant, wagging his head. "Both very good men," he added, without a trace of irony.

"It says in the Bible that a man cannot serve two masters," said the magistrate, sternly.

"I am Hindu, sir," explained the servant, with a sideways nod of the head.

Sighing, the magistrate ordered the man to load all the gifts onto a cart and deliver them back to Don Pedro's house. With a message.

"Tell him that I want none of his gifts or his business. Tell him also that I will put a stop to his nefarious trade and, if I catch him, he will hang."

A few hours later, the servant was seen dragging a creaking handcart piled high with sacks and bundles along the lonely road that led through coconut groves and winding tracks to Don Pedro's residence.

He did not return. There was no reply from Don Pedro and, after that, no further visits. But his temper was legendary and his rage at the magistrate's rejection of his terms can only be imagined.

It was the beginning of a struggle that lasted many months, each man striving for mastery over the other. Mr Diggory contrived to end Don Pedro's trade, leading armed patrols to disrupt the night-work of the smugglers, raiding illegal drinking dens, searching the houses of Don Pedro's associates. The courts were constantly in session and the gaols overflowed with criminals of all kinds; each one a small thread in Don Pedro's iniquitous web.

Eventually, it seemed that Don Pedro's power was broken. So it came as no surprise when the master-criminal - who had hitherto directed the activities of his accomplices from a distance - was apprehended during the burglary of a house. Apparently, the disruption of his trade had been so effective, that Don Pedro had been driven to commit a crime in person although, filled with bravado, he had performed the felony in broad daylight.

He was led in triumph to the court-house where, prior to appearing, he was kept under guard in a small ante-room. Dark and bare, its walls blackened with mildew, the room was lit by a single, barred window situated high overhead. It was barely large enough to admit a small child, even if it had been accessible from the ground, which made Don Pedro's escape all the more remarkable – or, should one say, suspicious.

The guards swore that they knew nothing of his disappearance until one, in an act of compassion, had opened the door to offer the prisoner a glass of water. The bars, loosened from their sockets and lying on the floor, told their own story.

Infuriated by the loss of his prisoner and deafened by the hubbub in the courtroom, Mr Diggory ordered several members of the local police to ride with him in pursuit of Don Pedro.

They galloped out of Negombo, along the single-track road, past the flickering sea flecked with tiny boats and the parched, yellow beach laced with drying nets; past palm trees and fishermen's huts; the cemetery with its low wall and white bunting; past rattling carts laden with rice; into the mottled light of coconut groves where the sun throws patterned shadows over the red earth.

On they rode, out into open country, where egrets wade through paddy fields and the air is mellow with the lowing of oxen. Until, at last, one of the men pointed to a narrow track.

"Along there, sir. That is where you will find him."

"Follow me!"

Mr Diggory spurred his horse forward down the track. So eager was he to recapture his prey that he did not look back to see if his men had followed him.

The track wound back and forth through densely overgrown scrubland, commonly called 'jungle'; a landscape characterised by tall grasses and stunted trees, the haunt of many wild and dangerous animals.

After a mile or so, the track opened out onto a clearing at whose heart stood a low, sprawling building, more like a stable in construction than a house. The place was silent and appeared to be deserted. Having ridden into the clearing, Mr Diggory looked behind him to see his men advancing at a slow trot.

"Hurry up!" he ordered impatiently. "What is detaining you?"

But at the entrance to the clearing, the men stopped, staring at him sullenly.

"What is the matter with you?" demanded Mr Diggory. "Are you afraid?"

One of the men nodded, but no word was spoken. They just sat there, watching Mr Diggory, their horses stamping and snorting. He had ridden far out into the countryside, to a desolate place far from help. He must have cursed himself for his recklessness.

"Damn you," he muttered. "I shall do the job myself."

Cantering up to the building, he tried to peer in through the dark windows.

"Hello," he shouted. "Hello."

As he passed one of the windows, a hand appeared and pointed a pistol at his back. As the bullet pierced Mr Diggory's heart, his horse reared and whinnied, throwing him to the ground.

This, at least, is the story told by the policemen when they arrived home that night with the magistrate's body slung over the back of his horse. And yet, there were some things that were never explained. His companions insisted that he had been shot by an unseen hand. Yet why was the murderer not apprehended? Why was there no attempt to give chase?

At about the time the murder took place, Don Pedro took care to show himself in Colombo, many miles away. So it could not have been him - at least, not personally - although, I often wonder if one of the magistrate's companions that day was not also the servant of two masters.

What is certain is the disastrous effect of her husband's death on Mrs Diggory. She lost the son that she was carrying a few days after giving birth, having already lost her small daughter the year before. Thus, in the space of a few months, she buried her husband and both children.

Grief-stricken, she refused to return to England. Instead, forced to quit the magistrate's residence and dismiss her servants, she sold most of her possessions and took a small house next to the cemetery where her husband and children were buried. I am told that she lives there still, immured with her grief, only venturing out to tend the graves of her loved ones.

***

After Mr Diggory's death, my mother found herself, once again, without work or a home. Having rented a single room off a dark courtyard, she tried to support us by taking in needlework but could not earn enough to sustain us.

Destitute and alone, she sought the company of men who, in her former life, she would have reviled. Eventually, she was taken on as a house-maid by Mr Landless, a minor clerk in the East India Company.

Still beautiful, she won his favour and, once more, became a 'native wife', gaining food and lodging for herself and her children. However, her position was little better than that of a servant and, in some ways, inferior; for her status was always uncertain and the work she performed, unpaid.

Being given to drink and ill-humour, Landless was not a kind man. At best, his attitude towards Neville and myself was grudging and, as we grew up, we did our best to stay out of his sight and the reach of his cane; a heavy Malacca stick tipped with silver that, when wielded in a drunken rage, would leave its mark for weeks.

You have often upbraided Neville for his propensity to clench his fist when angry, your reason being that you dislike this display of uncontrolled aggression. But, my dear, this is a misapprehension. Neville has learned to curb his temper through many hardships. What you observe is a sign of self-restraint, not lack of it.

When my mother, worn out and disillusioned, slipped from life, Neville and I were thrown on Landless's mercy. In a gesture that others regarded as generosity, but which sprang from a mercenary nature, he adopted us as his children.

In fact, we were his slaves, living in rags, sleeping on mats in the kitchen, cooking, cleaning and tending to his needs. His vicious temper was not improved by drink or the dwindling of his fortune. We became the butt of his sadistic humour.

"Landless you are and landless you shall be!"

And he had other, more painful taunts. He would beat me while Neville watched. Small though he was, on one occasion my brother tried to protect me; launching himself at Landless, biting and scratching, trying to restrain the hand that wielded the Malacca cane. So, to teach my brother a lesson, Landless beat me unconscious. After that, realising that intervention would only result in greater punishment, Neville learned to restrain himself; clenching his fists so that the nails bit into his flesh and drew blood.

We endured this cruelty for many years until Mr Landless died. But, even in death, he continued to torment us. The terms of his will dictated that we should be despatched to a land that we did not know and a man that we could not like.

Our new guardian, Mr Honeythunder was a humanitarian of the philosophical kind: his good deeds being a matter of conjecture, rather than action. It was only when Mr Honeythunder brought us to Cloisterham that we discovered true friendship.

But the disappearance of Edwin Drood cast a long shadow over us: in particular, my brother who, due to the connivance of one man and the stupidity of others, was nearly hanged.

It was only due to the good offices of yourself and Mr Grewgious, the lawyer, that Neville was finally cleared of the imputation of murder so diligently fostered by Edwin's uncle, the Cathedral choirmaster John Jasper.

The rest you know. But, for the sake of posterity and those who, in future, may wish to understand my present actions, it is worth reciting the facts.

Seized by an unwholesome passion for Edwin's fiancée, Rosa Bud, John Jasper sought a means of ridding himself of both young Mr Drood and my brother, both of whom he regarded as his rivals in love.

It was well-known at the time that my brother Neville and Edwin Drood were on bad terms. Jasper sought to profit from this by engineering a meeting that would lead to the disappearance of one and the incrimination of the other.

On Christmas Eve, Jasper invited Neville and Edwin to supper at his lodgings in the Cathedral gatehouse. With Jasper's subtle connivance, a previous meeting between these two young men had ended not only in hostility, but also in a violent show of temper by Neville.

However, on this occasion, Neville and Edwin resolved their differences and, leaving Jasper's rooms together, walked first to the Cathedral and then to the river which was in furious spate, it being a wild and blustery evening.

After staring into the whirling flood for a few minutes, the young men decided to return home, parting company at the door of your house where Neville was living as your pupil.

All this time, they had been observed by Jasper who had followed them from his lodgings, slipping unseen into the street from a small door that leads into the dark archway beneath the gatehouse. Wearing the dark pea-jacket and hat which he used to disguise himself for nocturnal sorties into the town, he crept softly through the shadows.

A dark and stealthy menace, he stalked the two young men to the Cathedral – eavesdropping on their conversation – then through Cloisterham's empty, storm-swept streets, down to the wide sweep of the river. He then followed them back to your house and, having watched them bid goodnight, he fled back to the gatehouse where, concealed beneath the arch, he lay in wait for Edwin.

As soon as his nephew came into view, Jasper stepped out of the shadow and hurried towards him, his expression one of deepest concern.

"Ned, Ned, dearest boy, where have you been? I have been worried almost to distraction."

At the word 'Ned', Edwin looked at his uncle askance. He had heard the name earlier that day from the lips of another who had warned him of a threat to one called 'Ned'. But the meeting had been a chance one and Edwin had dismissed the warning as the confused ramblings of a vagrant.

Seeing a flash of suspicion on his nephew's face, Jasper knew that he must act quickly. There must be no delay, no hesitation.

A few days earlier, with copious amounts of wine and liberal flattery, Jasper had inveigled the stonemason Durdles to conduct him on a secret tour of the Cathedral.

Telling Durdles that he wished to discover the mysteries and secret nooks of the great edifice, Jasper had plied the stonemason with alcohol, left him in a drunken stupor and briefly purloined his keys in order to unlock the crypt. The trap was set.

Now, with Edwin before him, Jasper made a show of avuncular concern, wrapping an arm around his nephew's shoulders and affecting that low, sweet voice which was his particular gift.

Edwin's fear was allayed and his low spirits leavened by the tale of a fantastical discovery. Not untruthfully, Jasper recounted how Durdles, by tapping with his hammer on the cloistral pavement, had discovered the long-forgotten tomb of a Norman prelate.

"Shall we not see him? Let us be the first. Come, dearest boy."

By this time, the rising wind of early evening had turned into a gale which, with the uncontrolled abandon of a gigantic child, was wilfully tearing branches from trees and flinging them across the sky. In the grasp of this preternatural force, Cloisterham was shaken to its ancient roots.

In that state of self-pity which attends a surfeit of

wine and rich food, Edwin ignored the whisperings of common sense and followed his uncle, eager for distraction and some shelter from the bone-biting chill.

Slipping silently through the Cathedral precincts - where nocturnal shadow lingers even in daylight - Jasper led his nephew between ancient headstones, their writing effaced by time and the restless elements; through the cloisters and down into the echoing crypt. Here, he enlisted his nephew's help in pushing back the lid of the stone sarcophagus.

Although it was too dark to see into the tomb, his uncle's vivid account had brought to life the vision of a prelate, magnificently preserved in all his medieval glory, a great golden crozier lying beside him, a ruby ring on his finger, his gloved hands pressed together in prayer. A captive to imagination, Edwin stared, transfixed, into the umbrous hollow.

"Wait while I fetch a candle," murmured Jasper, treading softly back into the shadow.

Leaning over the tomb, Edwin did not hear his uncle approaching quietly from behind. Wielding an iron candlestick, Jasper dealt his nephew a single, violent blow that crushed his skull, killing him outright.

Pausing only to remove the jewellery that Edwin

was accustomed to wear – his shirt-pin, watch and chain – Jasper tipped the corpse, fully-clothed, into the tomb and, with an effort that left him weak at the knees, pushed the stone cover back into place.

A few days later, having assisted in the dragging of the river that followed Edwin's disappearance and, having learned that the scope of this search would not be extended, Jasper threw the jewellery into the river some two miles away at Cloisterham Weir – a place in which you are accustomed to swim and from which you, yourself, retrieved the missing items.

In taking Edwin's shirt-pin, watch and chain, Jasper believed that he had removed the only items by which the body could be identified if, in the unlikely event, it were to be discovered at some future date. However, he had overlooked one thing. He did not know that, when Edwin returned to Cloisterham that Christmas, he carried a ring, supplied to him by Rosa Bud's guardian, Mr Grewgious.

This ring was bound up with tragedy, having been retrieved from the hand of Rosa's mother after she had drowned. It had subsequently been entrusted to Mr Grewgious's care with the intention of it being the ring with which Edwin proposed to Rosa (their fathers, being friends, having expressed a wish that their only children should marry each other).

At the beginning of that fateful Christmas week, Mr Grewgious had released the ring to Edwin for this purpose. However, if Edwin failed to commit himself to Rosa, Mr Grewgious had laid upon him an undertaking with these portentous words: *I charge you, by the living and the dead, to bring that ring back to me*!

So, Edwin carried the ring, in its box, in the breast-pocket of his coat, back to Cloisterham where he arranged to meet Rosa with the intention of asking her to be his wife. However, she pre-empted his proposal, suggesting that they put off all idea of marriage and that their relationship should, instead, be that of brother and sister. Relieved of the heavy duty placed on them by their parents, they embraced affectionately, observed by Jasper who, having heard nothing of their conversation, assumed that their engagement, so long awaited, had been confirmed.

Hesitation now sealed Edwin's fate. Unwilling to tell his uncle of their decision, he left Mr Grewgious to break the news to Jasper that the wedding would not take place. Thus, it was only after Edwin's murder that Jasper learned the truth: a discovery that induced in him a violent, nervous collapse.

However, undeterred by the wicked and senseless murder one young man, Jasper now set about encompassing the life of another: my brother, Neville.

Dear Septimus, it angers me to think how your decency and truthfulness were abused by that man to further his own wicked ends. For, after Edwin's disappearance, you revealed to Jasper what he had not known before: the depth of my brother's feelings for Rosa – the object of Jasper's insane passion.

Having long maligned Neville as part of his plan to lay the blame for Edwin's disappearance elsewhere, Jasper now redoubled his efforts. My brother's utter disgrace was but the first step in Jasper's plan to have him hung as a common criminal. And he may well have succeeded, had not Rosa, terrified by Jasper's advances some months after Edwin's disappearance, not run away to seek protection with her guardian, Mr Grewgious, convincing him of Jasper's inherent wickedness and strengthening the suspicions that he already entertained on that score.

Determined to uncover the truth, Mr Grewgious employed an enquiry agent in Cloisterham whose investigations soon bore fruit. On the evidence of an opium-seller whose den he frequented – and to whom he had confessed when intoxicated – John Jasper was arrested for his nephew's murder.

The tomb was opened and the body, much decomposed, was discovered. However, confident that he had removed all means of identification, Jasper denied any knowledge of the body – or that it was Edwin.

But he was undone. The ring, still in its box, was found in the corpse's breast-pocket and, having been identified by Mr Grewgious, proved beyond doubt that the body was that of Edwin.

Yet, Jasper still managed, in some degree, to elude justice. Faced with conclusive proof of his guilt and deprived of the drug on which he depended, he hanged himself from the bars of his cell with a long, black scarf that he had concealed upon him.

Edwin's body was duly buried within the consecrated ground of the Cathedral graveyard. Yet, despite the fact that all questions have been answered, there are many within the taverns and parlours of Cloisterham who still relish the mystery that accompanied his disappearance. And there are some who continue to profit from it, such as Durdles, the stonemason who, for the price of a pint of porter, will recount stories of ghostly screams and hauntings.

Although the facts have been laid bare, theories still abound and Neville, although absolved of guilt, is still the victim of whispering and petty prejudice. I do not think that he will ever be able to return to Cloisterham.

For myself, I have done with mystery. I want no more of it. Puzzles and conundrums hold no fascination for me. I abhor half-truths and the shadows which breed them. I cannot tolerate concealment and can only thrive in the pure sunlight of truth.

It is for that reason, my love, that I am making this journey back to the country of my birth. For there is still one unsolved mystery that torments me. My father's name. Out of loyalty, my mother always withheld it. But I cannot embark on a new life without a true knowledge of who I am.

I am, therefore, returning to Ceylon to see the only person who can unravel this enigma. Mrs Diggory. I am told that she is still living in the small house by the cemetery in which her husband and children are buried.

God willing she still has her wits about her and will be able to throw light on the mystery of my birth. She, alone, can answer the questions that have tormented me for years. Only then, when all my self-doubt has been laid to rest, will I be truly free to return and accept your offer of marriage.

For that reason, dear Septimus, I beg you most earnestly to pray for my success.

My heart will be, forever, yours,

Helena

About the Author

T. Thurai studied Medieval and Modern History at the University of London: both as an undergraduate at University College, then as a postgraduate (Master's Degree) at King's College.

She worked for 10 years as a journalist before re-training as a lawyer. When working with a City law firm, she co-wrote and edited a textbook on eCommerce law.

T. Thurai's first novel, *The Devil Dancers*, was published in 2011. It is set in 1950s Ceylon and follows the fortunes of its characters over a 4-year period as the country makes its painful transition into a nation-state following Independence.

Barley Bread and Cheese is T. Thurai's second work of fiction and her first collection of short stories. It was inspired by various treasures associated with Rochester Cathedral in Kent. The book takes its title from one of the ancient ordeals described in the *Textus Roffensis*.

T. Thurai has her own blog. She also writes articles and blogs for *Kent Life Magazine*.

Acknowledgments

My thanks to all the following for their generous support and encouragement:

The authorities, volunteers and congregation of Rochester Cathedral, especially the Rt Revd Mark Beach and Canon Jean Kerr; Sarah Sturt, Barbara Harris, Helen Theologitis, Luigi Marchini, Sue Donaldson, Gill Bromley, Caroline and Ian Atkinson, Jo and Peter Williams, Richard Bates, Eduardo Reyes, David Pickup, Diane Donovan, Gilda Puckett, Betty Poole, Rory Winter, Sergey Dyakonov, Ronni 'Aruni' Adams , Wimala and Chelvanayagam Menna, Mahan & Sharlene Thuraisingham, Uvindu Kurukulasuriya, Leland and Winnie Decambra, Christina Turnbull, Jean and Ed Fewins, Kingsley Rajah, Terrence Mano Ponniah, Aunty Chandra and Aruna Tissaweerasinghe, Lowri Stafford, Dinesh Tharmaratnam, Rachael Hale, Mary V James, Robert Richardson, Geraldine D'Amico, Maggie Harris, Maria, Franco, Barbara and Alessandro Biscardi, Georgia Reed, Jan and Roy Boorman, Jeanne Carlton, Jan Womack, Giselle Nunn, Jayne Wackett, Rosaleen Williams.

Appendix

The Broken Wing

Additional notes

Amble Links: A beach in Northumberland which features in the plot. I had a mental picture of this location before knowing what it was called – or even if it existed. Having described it in the story, I thought I had better check to see if such a landscape could be found in North-East England. Further research revealed Amble Links, a beach exactly matching that which I had visualised.

Kecks: A North Country term for underpants.

Jack

Naval connections

The sailor referred to in connection with Nelson was Walter Burke who served on HMS Victory at the Battle of Trafalgar in 1805. Burke died in 1815 aged 70. He is buried in the graveyard of All Saints church, Wouldham, near Rochester. A copy of Burke's entry in Wouldham's Burial Register can be viewed online at Medway City Archive's website (see below). This site also provides a unique account of the Battle of Trafalgar by another man from the Rochester area, Robert Sands, who served as a powder boy on HMS Temeraire. Altogether, some 99 Medway men fought in the Battle of Trafalgar.

The Catalpa Tree

The Catalpa tree mentioned in the story can be seen in the small garden near the west door of the Cathedral. It is estimated to be 150 years old. Also known as the Indian Bean Tree, this species originates from the USA. The botanist who first recorded the tree intended to name it after a local Indian tribe, the Catawba, but misspelt the name, writing it as 'Catalpa'.

The Wheel of Fortune

A historical note

Having been banished from the throne, King James II stayed at a house in Rochester High Street as the guest of Sir Richard Head before making his final departure for France on 23rd December 1688. The house can still be seen and is appropriately named 'Abdication House'.

Other examples of the Wheel of Fortune:

Medieval
A beautiful miniature from John Lydgate's 'Troy Book' and 'Siege of Thebes' can be found online at the British Library website: www.bl.uk . Lydgate (c. 1370 – 1450) was a monk at Bury St. Edmunds and a prolific poet. The miniature painting of the Wheel of Fortune in the illuminated manuscript of his work dates from c. 1460 – 1520.

Modern
The Wheel of Fortune also provides the subject of a painting by Pre-Raphaelite artist Edward Burne-Jones. Painted circa 1875-83, the painting now resides in the Musée d'Orsay Museum in Paris. An image and brief description of the painting can be found on the Museum's website at:
www.musee-orsay.fr

William of Perth

Historical notes

The following chronology places William's death in a wider historical context and may help to explain his emergence as a popular contemporary saint in medieval Rochester:

1170   Archbishop Thomas Becket is murdered in Canterbury Cathedral.

1173   Becket is canonised and Canterbury Cathedral becomes a major site of pilgrimage.

1179   Rochester Cathedral suffers the second of two devastating fires. The damage is so extensive that renovation continues into the next century.

1198   Newly-appointed Pope Innocent III proclaims a crusade.

1199   In order to finance the crusade, Innocent imposes a tax of one fortieth of income on all clergy: a heavy burden for religious communities already struggling with debt.

1199   A note in the *Textus Roffensis* records an inquisition into Rochester Priory's debts.

c.1201 On pilgrimage to Canterbury, William of Perth stays in Rochester and is murdered as he leaves the town. Benedictine monks recover his body and bury it in the Cathedral. William's tomb attracts many pilgrims.

1256   The Bishop of Rochester Lawrence de San Martino obtains William's canonisation. He becomes St. William of Rochester, patron of adopted children.

Medieval shrines – particularly those of popular contemporary saints – provided an important source of income for religious institutions. William's shrine was no exception and the money it raised would have helped to fund the long-term restoration of the Cathedral following extensive fire damage in the 12th century.

Sadly, William's shrine no longer exists. Like that of Thomas Becket, it fell foul of Henry VIII and was destroyed during the Dissolution of the Monasteries in 1538. However, the Pilgrims' Steps that led to William's shrine can still be seen in the North Quire Aisle. Heavily worn down by many feet, they bear witness to his popularity among medieval pilgrims.

The Nova Legenda Anglie

The *Nova Legenda Anglie* was a compilation of the lives of British saints. Initially entitled *Sanctilogium Angliae, Walliae, Scotiae, et Hiberniae*, it was written by John of Tynemouth c. mid-14th century and recorded the lives of 156 saints. Subsequently re-named the *Nova Legenda Anglie*, the text was edited and re-arranged in the 16th century by Wynkyn de Worde who added a number of new saints' lives, including that of William of Perth. The first printed edition of the work appeared in 1516, the work of de Worde who was Caxton's apprentice and successor.

While the *Nova Legenda Anglie* accuses William's son David of patricide, there is nothing to substantiate this allegation. In fact, the account of William's life was added to the *Legenda* over three centuries after his death.

In my view, the discovery of a local culprit would have had serious implications for Rochester's burgeoning pilgrimage industry. Far better to blame an outsider; someone unconnected with the area. It may be that, far from being a murderer, David was simply a scapegoat.

The Textus Roffensis

Sadly, the *Textus* is not on public view owing to its delicate state. However, a digitised copy is available from Medway City Archive at: http://cityark.medway.gov.uk/

The Cinnamon Peeler's Daughter

The Ceylon Connection

Having spent nine years researching and writing *The Devil Dancers*, a novel set in 1950s Ceylon, I was intrigued by Dickens's reference to that country in *The Mystery of Edwin Drood*. This, for me, was the real mystery. I wondered what had inspired him. One might have expected a reference to India – or even the North West frontier – but why Ceylon?

I made several trips to Rochester and spent a considerable amount of time in the Cathedral reading memorial plaques. I thought that these might provide a clue as Dickens had made a number of references to memorial tablets and inscriptions in his novel: for example, the inscription for Mrs. Sapsea's monument and the inscription over the door of Mr. Grewgious's lodgings.

Dickens would also have known of the close connection between the Royal Engineers at Chatham and Rochester Cathedral. Some 25 memorial plaques pay tribute to soldiers from this Regiment who died in far-flung corners of the British Empire. In Dickens's novel, both Edwin Drood and his father were described as engineers.

Owing to this, I was certain that the Cathedral must hold the clue to Dickens's obscure reference to Ceylon. But I was wrong.

The most probable link between Dickens and Ceylon was provided by another memorial; a gravestone in a small Anglican cemetery in Kandy, Sri Lanka (formerly Ceylon). This commemorates William Charles MacReady (d. 1871) a civil servant and linguist whose father, the celebrated actor William, was known to Dickens.

By this time, I had studied a number of memorial tablets and inscriptions. To my surprise, they provided a rich commentary on the lives of soldiers and civil servants who served abroad. For example, the graveyard at Kandy provided the extraordinary tale of Captain James McGlashan who trekked from one end of the island to the other.

Closer to home, a chance visit to the parish church of Chilham, Kent, revealed the extraordinary account of Frederick Lacy Dick, a district magistrate who was assassinated in Ceylon in 1847. The story on his commemorative tablet struck a chord with me.

It was not only relevant to the period in which Dickens lived and worked, but it provided a fascinating insight into the life of a British civil servant in Ceylon. Although Dickens may never have seen this particular memorial, it provided the kind of story I was looking for and I used it as the basis for the character of Mr. Diggory in my short story.

Historical sources

1. Captain James McGlashan (d. 1817) is buried in the British Garrison Cemetery near to the Temple of the Tooth in Kandy, Sri Lanka (formerly Ceylon). His extraordinary trek from Trincomalee on Ceylon's North-East coast to Kandy is a matter of record. His tombstone was transferred to this cemetery in the 1880s.

2. The story of Mr. Diggory was inspired by the memorial tablet to Frederick Lacy Dick (d. 1847) in Chilham parish church, Kent. This monument records in extraordinary

detail the circumstances of Mr. Dick's assassination "by an unseen hand" when he was serving as a District Magistrate at Negombo, Ceylon. The story was also reported in The Times (October 26, 1847).

3. Rochester Cathedral (aka Cloisterham) contains over 25 memorial tablets dedicated to members of the Corps of Royal Engineers. This building has had a close relationship to military engineers since the time of Bishop Gundulf (d. 1108) who not only re-built the Cathedral but oversaw construction work on Rochester Castle. Many of the Royal Engineers' memorial plaques tell stories of the bravery, sickness and sheer bad luck of soldiers who died overseas when the British Empire was at the height of its power in the 19th century. The men who died were extremely young by our standards and the commemorative inscriptions provide a fascinating, if sobering, insight not just into the deaths, but also into the lives and work of those employed in various overseas postings. These monuments also give an idea of the geographical extent of the Empire during this period, with references to places as diverse as Afghanistan, Africa and Canada.

4. Dickens wanted to be buried in Rochester Cathedral's graveyard. However, his wishes were ignored and he was interred in Poets' Corner at Westminster Abbey. His connection with Rochester Cathedral is commemorated by a wall plaque in the South Quire Transept.

ROCHESTER CATHEDRAL

Further information about the Cathedral can be obtained from: www.rochestercathedral.org
Or:
The Chapter Office
Garth House, The Precinct
Rochester, Kent, ME1 1SX
United Kingdom,

Also by this author:

THE DEVIL DANCERS

A historical novel set in 1950s Ceylon

by T. Thurai

FOLLOWING Independence from the British, Ceylon's future looks bright. A new prime minister is creating a modern nation. But his legacy is an unexpected one. The deals that brought him to power turn into a time-bomb and the country is contorted by bloody race riots.

A widening rift divides Tamils and Sinhalese destroying communities. Neighbour turns on neighbour. As the terror increases, many lives are transformed.

In this atmosphere of violence and uncertainty, relationships fracture and families fragment reflecting the wider political turmoil. Yet, weaving its way through the mayhem is a single, twisted thread: the story of Neleni and Arjun.

AVAILABILITY:

Paperback: Amazon, Dawson Books, Bertram's, author's website (below)

eBooks: Kindle (via Amazon) and ePub (via Kobo)

FURTHER INFORMATION: can be found on the author's website at www.thedevildancers.com

Reviews and commentary:

THE DEVIL DANCERS

"An amazing historical novel, love story, political novel. Incredibly rich, full of characters and adventures. Quite an amazing novel for a first novel. Wonderful writing."
Geraldine D'Amico – Curator Folkestone Book Festival

"Ceylon in the mid-1950s was a pivotal time, with forces erupting that would challenge and change the country's direction, ultimately creating a 25-year civil war that would become a way of life for many. ... T. Thurai's writing imparts information deftly in a manner that assumes no prior familiarity with Ceylonese culture or history ... a powerful saga of love, violence, and perseverance."
Diane Donovan, West Coast editor, MidWest Book Review, USA

"Thurai's debut teems with characters navigating the social, political and spiritual realities of 1950s Ceylon, in what is now Sri Lanka. ... powerful insight into post-colonial politics and the beginnings of Sri Lanka's violent war ... Sultry romance, tense politicking and colorful mythmaking combine for a broad, engaging novel."
Kirkus Reviews, USA

"This enjoyable work brings a neglected period alive. I look forward to her next books."
David Pickup, book reviewer for the UK Law Society Gazette